GAME FACE

Also by Sylvia Gunnery in the
Lorimer Sports Stories series
Out of Bounds
Personal Best

GAME FACE

Sylvia Gunnery

James Lorimer & Company Ltd., Publishers
Toronto

James Lorimer & Company Ltd., Publishers acknowledges the support of the Ontario Arts Council. We acknowledge the financial support of the Government of Canada through the Canada Book Fund for our publishing activities. We acknowledge the support of the Canada Council for the Arts which last year invested $24.3 million in writing and publishing throughout Canada. We acknowledge the Government of Ontario through the Ontario Media Development Corporation's Ontario Book Initiative.

Library and Archives Canada Cataloguing in Publication
Gunnery, Sylvia
Game face / Sylvia Gunnery.
(Sports stories)
Issued also in electronic format.
ISBN 978-1-4594-0376-5 (bound).--ISBN 978-1-4594-0375-8 (pbk.)
I. Title. II. Series: Sports stories (Toronto, Ont.)
PS8563.U575G34 2013 jC813'.54 C2012-908237-6

James Lorimer & Company Ltd.,
Publishers
317 Adelaide Street West, Suite
#1002
Toronto, ON, Canada
M5V 1P9
www.lorimer.ca

Distributed in the United States by:
Orca Book Publishers
P.O. Box 468
Custer, WA U.S.A.
98240-0468

Printed and bound in Canada
Manufactured by Friesens Corporation in Altona, Manitoba, Canada in
February 2013.
Job #82154

For Barb, Ava, and Benson

CONTENTS

1 BACK IN ROCKETS TERRITORY

Jay Hirtle got off the bus in front of Richmond Academy and looked around. He may as well have been stepping onto the moon. Nothing felt familiar.

A few people hung out by the bicycle racks, some sprawled on the lawns, and others hugged or gave high-fives to friends they hadn't seen since June. The sun was beating down like summer vacation wasn't over.

Though he was now in grade nine, Jay had that same tight feeling in his gut he'd had on his first day of grade seven.

"Welcome back, Jay! Great to see you here again!" Mr. Haley, the principal, was doing his usual rounds, greeting everyone like they were arriving at a picnic instead of starting another school year. "How's your family doing?"

"Uh, pretty good, sir."

"You've all been through a lot, with the fire and then moving to Centreville. Not easy stuff. But now your house is fixed and you're back here with all your friends."

As if on cue, Colin Hebb got off the bus. Jay didn't miss the dirty look Colin gave him before turning and heading in the other direction.

"Nothing's really the same," said Jay solemnly.

"Your basketball team understands why you did what you did." Mr. Haley obviously hadn't seen the scowl on Colin's face.

"Maybe. At least some of them."

"Once you're wearing your Rockets' jersey again, no one will even remember you played a few games for Centreville last season."

"That was so weird. Especially the game against the Rockets."

"I know you tried to give the Cougars your very best in that game. I was there. But now you're back in Rockets territory. Go find your buddies and get back in the stream of things. It'll be like you never left." He gave Jay's shoulder a reassuring pat, and then turned his attention to a group of new students clustered together.

But Jay wasn't reassured.

The sound of a basketball bouncing caught his attention. Tyler and Cory, two of Jay's old teammates, were shooting baskets at the outside hoops.

"Jay!" Finn, another Rockets player, left the guys by the bike racks and walked over to Jay. "How's it goin'? Wanna shoot some baskets?"

"Uh . . . sure." Finn obviously wasn't holding any grudges. Maybe Mr. Haley was right. Maybe Jay had no reason to feel so alien. He had played with these guys for almost two seasons, so why get all paranoid about a couple of games he'd played for another school?

Tyler's shot slipped through the net and Cory caught the ball.

"How about two-on-two?" asked Finn. "Me and Jay against you guys?"

Cory missed the not-too-friendly look on Tyler's face. He tossed the ball to Finn. "Sure," he said. "You start."

Finn bounced the ball evenly, keeping the hoop in sight and watching Jay move easily around Cory. Tyler stepped in to block the pass. Finn pivoted. Jay switched directions and was there for the bounce pass. He jumped for the shot. The ball rolled around the rim and fell outside.

Tyler was under the basket for the rebound. His slam dunk brought a few cheers from the small crowd that had gathered. "That's it for me," Tyler said. "I'm outta here."

Finn retrieved the ball. "What's up? We just got started."

"Gotta go find Colin," said Tyler.

Finn and Cory didn't seem to know what was going on, but Jay did. Tyler was likely Colin's best friend now, and that meant he'd know why Colin was avoiding Jay. The tight feeling in Jay's stomach pinched even tighter.

"We can get someone else," said Finn.

"No, you guys keep playing," said Jay. "I got something I need to do. Thanks anyway." He went past the small crowd, walked over to the open door at the back of the gym, and stepped inside.

There, in the wide expanse of the gymnasium, everything was familiar. The waxy smell of the freshly polished floor. The gleaming red, yellow, and green lines. The wooden bleachers folded against both sides, ready to be pulled out for game action. Championship banners hung high along the walls — track and field, volleyball, soccer, basketball, wrestling, badminton, hockey.

Jay walked across the basketball court until he stood at centre. In his imagination, he could hear the sound of a basketball pounding against the floor. Quick shouts and the squeak and scuff of sneakers. Then loud cheers as the basketball dropped solidly through the hoop.

It was a no-brainer — basketball was Jay's number-one reason for going to school.

He looked around at all the banners. It had been a while since the Rockets had won the Western Region Junior Boys basketball championship. For the last three years, the Centreville Cougars had claimed that banner. *Maybe this year, things would change,* Jay thought. *Why not?*

Silently, Jay made a promise to do whatever he could to help the Rockets bring home that championship banner. He'd work on his game — offence, defence, shooting, dribbling, passing, receiving. All of it.

And he'd stay positive. Nothing would sidetrack him from this goal.

Through the large window on one side of the gym, he saw Coach Willis in his office, flipping through charts and lists, wearing his Rockets' coach's sweater as usual, his whistle hanging around his neck like he never took it off.

Jay quietly left before Coach Willis had time to look up from his papers and notice him standing in the gym by himself.

A half-hour later, Jay was in homeroom, slouched in his desk, ready for school to officially begin. He'd have to listen to the same rules he'd heard at the beginning of every school year. Then there'd probably be a speech about Grade Nines being seniors and setting a good example for the younger grades. The teacher would likely talk about graduation as if it was next week and not ten months away.

"Good morning, class!" his homeroom teacher said enthusiastically. "This is a very special day for many reasons, not the least of which is that all of you are beginning your senior year at Richmond Academy! And today, we are welcoming a new student — not only to our class, but to our school, our community, and to Canada. Kyung Yi and his parents have recently arrived from the city of Seoul in South Korea. Welcome, Kyung!" She began to clap and almost everyone picked up the applause.

In a seat at the back of the room, a slim guy wearing dark-rimmed glasses smiled hesitantly. Everything he was wearing — grey T-shirt, jeans, sneakers — looked new. His thick black hair was streaked with bright orange. As the applause ended and everyone faced the teacher again, Jay noticed how fast the new guy's smile faded. He definitely looked like a person who was half the entire earth away from where he was born and where he'd lived his whole life until now.

Jay turned his attention back to the droning list of first-day instructions.

At noon, he headed to the cafeteria to grab a sandwich. Just outside the cafeteria door, he almost collided with Colin and Tyler.

"How's things with the Cougars?" asked Colin.

"Drop it, Colin," said Jay.

"Oh, right. Drop it. Like you never played for Centreville last year. Like you're not a traitor."

"Gimme a break," said Jay. "*A traitor.* That's so stupid."

"You calling me stupid?" asked Colin loudly.

"How's it going, boys?" Mr. Haley came out of the cafeteria and stopped beside them. "Everything okay here?"

Tyler and Colin said nothing, both avoiding eye contact with the principal.

"I was just going to get a sandwich," said Jay.

"Well, it's too nice a day to be inside all lunch hour.

Colin and Tyler, if you two have eaten, then get out there."

As he walked into the cafeteria, Jay looked back over his shoulder at Colin and Tyler heading toward the main entrance. Mr. Haley was watching them, too.

The new student from Jay's homeroom was standing in front of the cafeteria counter, reading the words on a small chalkboard: *Today's Special — Cheese Pizza.*

"The pizza's not bad," said Jay. "But the sandwiches are better."

"I like pizza with more than just cheese," said Kyung.

"Me too."

Silence fell between them as the cafeteria line moved forward. Jay tried to think of something to say that wouldn't sound lame. "So, how do you like Canada so far?" *Lame.*

"It is very good. Richmond is a very small town, but very nice."

More silence.

"Anyone show you around the school yet?"

"Yes," said Kyung. "Mr. Haley showed the school to my parents and me yesterday."

"Well, if you have questions, just ask."

"I have one question."

"Yeah?"

"What is your name?"

Jay gave a quick laugh. "Right. Should've thought of that! I'm Jay."

"I am Kyung."

Jay tried to say the syllables the same way Kyung did, like *key* and then *oong*. "Ky . . . ung."

"Yes. That is right."

"So, after we get our stuff, we can eat outside if you want," said Jay.

Kyung nodded his head and smiled. "Okay."

When they were settled on the lawn with their sandwiches, Jay recalled what he'd been thinking when Kyung was first introduced in homeroom. "Must be pretty weird living here in Nova Scotia with Korea so far away."

The expression on Kyung's face made him regret saying it. "I mean, it'd be exciting and all that. Travelling so far."

"My parents want to make a new life in Canada. We will become Canadian citizens." Though Kyung's voice sounded confident, there was sadness mixed in.

Jay took a bite of his sandwich, almost afraid to say anything else. He realized that, for Kyung, it wasn't just Korea that was far away — it was friends and family and all the things that made his life normal. Jay thought about how his own family had left Richmond and lived in Centreville for a while. But Centreville wasn't even an hour away. It was still in Nova Scotia, not on the other side of the world.

"You into sports?" Jay asked.

"Yes. Lots of sports."

"What's your favourite?"

"Basketball."

"Hey, same here! Who's your team?"

"Knights."

"Knights? Do you mean Knicks? New York Knicks?"

"SK Knights."

"Who are they?"

"Seoul is my city. SK Knights are my team."

Jay was still puzzled.

"You think Korea has no basketball," said Kyung. "We have basketball. KBL — Korean Basketball League. Like the NBA."

"I just never —"

"You don't know Korea," Kyung said quietly. "Many people don't know Korea. It's okay. I am used to it."

But it was obvious he wasn't used to it at all.

* * *

When he turned the corner of his street, Jay could see his little brother, Sam, doing wheelies on his bike, showing off. "Hey!" Jay shouted.

Sam dipped the front wheel back onto the side-walk and raced toward his brother. He sped past, then slammed on the brakes, skidding sideways.

"You got a licence for that weapon?"

"Mom's at the hospital because a baby's being

borned. Dad's making mac 'n' cheese."

"I'm famished. Hope he's making a truck load."

"A train load."

"A cargo ship load."

"A space shuttle load."

They turned into their driveway and walked around the back of the house. Rudy was in his chain-link kennel, wagging his tail and grinning that German Shepherd grin, his tongue sticking out.

"You put your bike away," said Jay, "and I'll take Rudy in the house. Don't forget to—"

"I know. Don't forget to lock the garage."

After supper, Jay was in his room when a light *tap-tap* sounded on his door. "May I come in?"

"Sure, Dad."

"Got something you might be interested in." He handed Jay a long cardboard tube.

Jay pulled the cap off the tube and a poster slid out. When he unfurled it, he was amazed. There was Spud Webb wearing the Atlanta Hawks red and white basketball jersey. An action shot. One of his famous jumps — his arm high above the hoop a split second before making a slam dunk. The crowd in the background looked stunned by what they saw.

"Spud Webb," said Jay.

"Slam Dunk Competition, 1986."

"Look how high the guy is."

"A forty-two inch vertical jump."

"He's flying."

"Maybe find a place to put up the poster. Inspire your game."

Jay grinned. "This is going right above my desk."

"Need any help?"

"No. I got it. Thanks."

His father left the room and closed the door quietly behind him.

When the poster was in place, Jay opened his laptop. In seconds, there was Spud Webb on YouTube. Running up the court, making that jump and his amazing back hand dunk, then hanging on to the hoop after his delivery. The crowd screaming. Players giving double high-fives. Number 4, Spud Webb. Five feet, seven inches — same height as Jay. The guy looked like a kid beside all those giants. Jay watched the video over and over and over.

Just as he was about to shut down his computer, Jay thought of something else. He Googled "SK Knights basketball." Partway down the screen was a thumbnail for a movie clip. It was fast paced and hyped, animation mixed with still shots in black and white and game-action video clips in colour, with everything bursting through a black wall. Too cool.

He clicked on another site and found a video showing the last few minutes of a KBL champion-ship game. The announcer was speaking Korean, but it didn't matter. It was basketball — everything was the same. The look on the player's face when the ref made a call against his team was the look any guy would have when the score's tied, the game's almost over, and your team gets a bad call.

When the action started again, it showed a player on the red team weaving in through defence before anyone could stop him. He jumped and the ball dropped in. With seconds spinning away on the clock, the coach of the team in green was shouting and waving from the sidelines to get the action back down the court. Greens tried for the tie shot. A miss. The ball hit the floor and the game was over.

Great basketball action! thought Jay.

And he knew the Richmond Rockets would claim the championship banner, no problem, if they could execute just one of those amazing moves.

2 TRYOUTS AND TROUBLE

Jay needed time alone. Time to do warm-up laps around the gym. Time to think. It was the beginning of his last basketball season with the Rockets and he had a promise to keep.

Most guys trying out for the basketball team weren't even in the changing room yet. Jay had bolted from his last class, slammed his books inside his locker, grabbed his duffle bag, and made it to the locker room even before the Grade Sevens from the last gym class were out of there.

For weeks, he'd been anxious for basketball tryouts to begin. Anxious in an excited way because basketball was the top reason to be at school. And anxious in a worried way because, although he was feeling good being at Richmond, not everyone on his old team was glad he was back. Colin and Tyler had been hanging out together and pretty much ignoring Jay. But that wouldn't be so easy for them once basketball season started.

Jay's breathing was even and his stride was long as he jogged past the coach's office. Coach Willis looked up from his computer and smiled. Jay raised his hand in response.

Soon, a few guys came out of the locker room and, and taking the hint from Jay, started running. The first one to pass him was Colin. He didn't look back.

Kyung sprinted to catch up to Jay.

"Hey, Kyung, how's it goin'?"

"Good, because now we get to play basketball."

"You got that right."

They continued around the gym together, Jay slowing just a bit to keep his pace even with Kyung's.

Coach Willis blew his whistle. "Okay! Over here! Listen up, guys." He waited for everyone to find a spot on the floor and settle down. "Lots of familiar faces here in front of me. That's good. And a few new ones. That's good, too. Everyone trying out for this basketball team has as good a chance as everyone else. Work together in these tryouts like you're already a team. Basketball's a team sport. If you're a basketball player, you're a team player."

Jay looked over at Kyung and gave a thumbs-up. Kyung smiled, but it faded fast, reminding Jay of the first day of school. Things hadn't changed much for Kyung in the weeks since then. He was still quiet, still seemed to be just outside of everything.

"Now, before we get into drills and strategies, I need

to see what you guys can do," said the coach. "Let's play a few scrimmages. Number off in threes. Ones in green pinnies against threes in blue pinnies. Twos will sit out the first game." When they started to number off, Coach stopped them. "Hold on there, Tyler. Your number is two, not three. No rigging the teams. Check your attitude."

When the numbering was finished, Jay walked over to the bench to join the rest of the twos. He sat next to Kyung, who was adjusting the safety strap on his dark-rimmed glasses.

"Ready to show Coach Willis how you play like the SK Knights?"

Kyung didn't laugh. "I hope I get to be a player on this team. It means a lot to me." He put on his glasses and pushed his hair off his forehead. "In Korea, I always play my best. But now I am not positive I will play my best."

"Don't sweat it. Basketball's basketball. Doesn't matter where you play, it's all the same. Rules, moves, everything."

"Yes, that is true. But the team is not the same. I am not —"

A sudden shout drew their attention to the court.

"Over here!" It was Colin, positioned for a layup and wide open. The pass was high and slow, allowing time for defence to scramble into place and make the block. The ball was tipped away and the play reversed direction. Jay caught the look on Colin's face and knew exactly what he'd just muttered.

Coach Willis was obviously a lip reader, too. He blasted his whistle. "Substitution! Colin, you're out! David, you're in!"

Colin sat on the bench beside Jay, the only space available. He didn't say anything, just leaned forward with his elbows on his knees.

If this were last year, Jay might've said something to Colin, like, "Tough call" or "Don't sweat the small stuff." Jay could picture Colin sitting back and muttering some joke like, "What's Willis got against Latin?" They'd both have smirks on their faces and would have another laugh about it in the locker room after practice.

Lots of things change in a year, thought Jay.

A second basket was scored, and Coach Willis stopped the action. "Let's switch things up. Twos against ones!"

"Here we go!" Jay said to Kyung. "SK Knights! Let's do it!"

"Colin, you're back in," said Coach Willis. "Try to keep it that way. Tyler and Colin, take the jump at centre." He held the ball in the air and waited until the players found their positions. Then he blew the whistle and tossed the ball.

Tyler tipped the ball away from Colin, but it hit the floor and rolled out of bounds.

Coach Willis stopped the game. "Let's try that again.

I want to see a plan for that basketball. Where's it going? Who's receiving?" He tossed the ball.

Colin's leap was successful and the ball was solidly received. Tyler made up for the miss by a quick and tight defence that stopped the player with the ball. The guy fumbled and the ball bounced free. Tyler grabbed it and pivoted. Then he slowed down the action with a steady dribble on the spot, his arm held out against any move from his guard.

Jay headed for the basket. Tyler saw him and made the pass. Jay caught the ball and dribbled twice before he came up against a two-man block. He quickly tossed the ball over their heads to Kyung, who was under the basket. Kyung received the pass, hesitated, then aimed. The ball rolled on the edge of the rim and teetered, then fell lazily through the hoop. Kyung raised his arms in victory.

"Two!" shouted Jay.

The coach blew his whistle. "Okay. Okay. Let's do a mental replay and remember what we just saw. Who can tell me the precise moment this two-pointer started?"

"Tyler blocked the pass and stole the ball."

"Right. Exactly right. Then what?"

"He threw it to Jay."

"No. That came later. What happened before that?"

Everyone searched their minds for every detail of the play.

"I slowed things down," said Tyler.

"That's it. You slowed things down. And tell us why you did that."

"To avoid a scramble. So guys could plan their moves."

"Right." The coach looked around to make sure everyone was listening, then he gave his lecture. "This is basketball. It's not a game of speed. It's a game of moves. Intelligent moves. Basketball players anticipate. Basketball players read the defence. They do not throw the ball away. That's why there are times when the action's gotta slow down." He turned back to Tyler. "Great ball handling, Tyler. And you used your team. That's what we want. Thank you. And Kyung, don't give your opponent an opportunity — even two seconds' worth — to move in and block your shot. You were lucky this time." He blew the whistle. "Ones, the ball is yours. Take it out under the basket. Let's play this game."

Jay glanced at Kyung. He could see that Kyung's victory mood had been zapped by what Coach Willis had said. Who'd want their coach to call a shot lucky? No one. Especially a guy who's worried his game's off because he's playing with guys he hardly knows.

"Let's review give-and-go," said Coach Willis. "Cory, you start."

"It's a basic offensive play. You fake direction to lose your guard."

"Where's the ball? What's the sequence? Jay?"

"You have the ball. You pass it and cut to the basket to receive the ball back again."

"Where's the fake Cory was talking about?"

"Pass. Then fake. Then cut to the basket."

"Right."

"And make the shot count," Jay added.

"Exactly. Let's see this in action. Jay, you're in the middle. Cory, you're over at the side. Show us what you got."

Everyone moved off the court except Jay and Cory.

Jay threw a solid chest pass to Cory, faked to the right and then made a quick diagonal left toward the basket. He missed Cory's return pass and the ball bounced out of bounds.

"One more time," said the coach. "Keep your eye on the ball, Jay."

Jay spun the ball between his fingertips, trying to concentrate on his next moves. This was just a demo. No defence to stop him. No surprise moves. He should have caught Cory's pass.

He took a deep breath, made a rapid pass to Cory, then faked left. He switched direction and ran down the middle of the key. Cory's pass found its mark and Jay jumped for the layup. But the ball overshot the hoop and dropped. Jay's heart sank. With all eyes on him, he'd just messed up two plays.

Cory retrieved the ball on the second bounce, dribbled to the other end of the court, and made his shot.

It missed. He scrambled for the ball and started to aim his overhead pass.

"Okay. That's the general idea," said Coach Willis. His disappointment was unmistakable. "Thank you, gentlemen. Tyler, explain the drill set-up."

Jay sat back down, hoping the sinking feeling he had would soon evaporate. Why should he be that uptight trying out for a team he'd already played on for two years?

"Well, there's two lines and three basketballs," said Tyler. "One line's down the middle and one's over at the side. The first three guys in the middle line have the basketballs."

"Brendan, explain the action."

"The first guy in the middle — he's at the top of the key — passes to the first guy in the other line. Then the middle guy does a quick fake and changes direction. He receives the return and goes in for a layup. The other guy gets the rebound and makes a fast break all the way down to the other basket. He scores, gets his rebound, and overhead passes to the last guy in the middle line. Then he goes to the middle line and waits his turn. They switch up, so the first guy's over in the other line now."

"And while all this is going on, we just stand around watching the action?" asked the coach.

"The next two guys in line start the play as soon as the key's free," said Brendan. "But everyone else watches."

"Right. The action doesn't stop. Got that? Good. Let's see two lines. Finn, you're first in the middle. Steve, you're first on the side."

When everyone was in their places, Jay cautiously looked to see who he'd be doing the drill with. He was fourth. The fourth guy in the opposite line was Kyung. Good. It'd be easy doing the drill with him. No pressure. As he counted back, he saw Colin switch places in line so he'd do the drill with Tyler. Those guys weren't going to chance teaming up with someone who wasn't rock-solid.

The action moved fast, and in just minutes, Kyung passed the ball to Jay. He fumbled, but recovered and made the return. Kyung grabbed the ball, pivoted, and jumped for his shot. The ball smacked against the backboard and slammed to the floor. Jay retrieved it and made a fast break to the other end of the gym. His layup was good, but they had lost too much time. No one was watching. Jay got his rebound and threw the ball to the last guy in the middle line. As he jogged back into position, he gave himself a pep talk. *Take it cool. Play like normal.*

Inside the key, a ball had just landed in Colin's hands. He went up for the shot and the ball swished through the hoop. Tyler was there for the rebound. In seconds, he was under the basket at the other end of the court. His layup was dead-on and his overhead pass to the guy at the end of the middle line was strong. Jay could see

Coach Willis making mental notes.

The lines kept moving as the drill continued. Jay suddenly realized that Kyung wasn't opposite him.

"Hey, Brendan," he said quietly. "Mind if we switch places? My fumble threw Kyung off last time. I'd like to give it another try."

Kyung was studying the action in the key as Jay quickly stepped behind Brendan.

Soon they were both at the front of their lines. Jay's pass was low. Kyung grabbed the ball and made the return pass. Jay dribbled closer to the basket, but his balance was off as he jumped for the shot. The ball tapped the edge of the backboard and fell. Kyung got the rebound and started down the court.

As he headed to the sideline, Jay could see that Coach Willis was not impressed with what he had seen. If the coach was making any mental notes now, they weren't going to be positive ones.

Again, Tyler and Colin tried to make sure they were opposite each other, but this time, Coach Willis caught the move. "Tyler, back of the line."

Jay realized that it put him opposite Colin. His heart lurched.

In seconds, Colin was at the head of the line, holding the ball. The key was clear. He made a bounce pass to Jay, faked left and ran toward the basket. Jay's return was quick but had too much power behind it. The ball flew past Colin, hit the floor, and bounced uselessly out of bounds. Without even looking at Jay, Colin walked out of the key to the end of the line. Jay hustled over, picked up the ball and completed the drill.

Coach Willis blew the whistle. "Time to work on dribbling! Get a partner and pick a defined area. Use the key, the three-point line, any defined area. Ball goes outside the area, you switch up offence and defence."

Kyung picked up a basketball and walked over to Jay. "You are not playing your best basketball. Like me."

"Just off my game today."

"For what reason?"

"Who knows?" Jay said defensively. "Same reason you're off, maybe."

"For me, everyone is new. That is the number-one reason. I am not used to playing with all these guys. You should not be off your game because you have already played for the Rockets."

Jay frowned.

"Kyung. Jay. Come on, fellas!" shouted Coach Willis. "Let me see some action here."

Kyung tossed the ball to Jay. "I will be defence."

Jay went into the centre circle and started to dribble, keeping his back to Kyung.

"That's it, Jay. Protect the ball," said Coach Willis. "No fouling. No pushing away. Good. Stay with him, Kyung. Force the ball outside that circle. Jay, keep your head up."

Jay pivoted. Kyung kept his defence tight. Jay lost

his balance and the ball went outside the centre circle.

"Switch it up. Kyung, you're offence." Coach Willis moved away to give tips to a couple of players at the top of the key.

Soon he blew his whistle again. "Okay. Now, let's look at triple threat."

★ ★ ★

When practice finally ended, Jay's hair was stuck to his forehead and sweat trickled down his neck. He lifted the edge of his T-shirt and wiped his face.

"Last season," said Coach Willis, "our team came close, very close, to owning that spot at the regionals. We played some tough games. And even though some of our guys have moved on to high school, we still got plenty of solid talent for the tough games we'll be playing this season. Like Colin, over there — MVP."

Everyone gave a noisy round of applause.

Coach let the applause fade, then added, "Though he almost messed up on that honour." He waited to let the idea sink in. "I'm not saying anything you don't already know, Colin. There's no room for temper or ego out on the basketball court. You did pull through for us. No question. But remember that no one's infallible. And everyone relies on everyone else. This is no one-man show."

Jay glanced at Colin to see how he was taking the lecture. Coach Willis didn't pull any punches. Everyone knew that. But being singled out like that had to be embarrassing. Colin stared down at his sneakers for a couple of seconds, then looked over at Tyler and raised his eyebrows as if to say, "So what?"

"These may be tryouts," said Coach Willis, "but I want to see teamwork, same as in any basketball game. Play like you're already on the Rockets and it's likely you'll find yourself wearing a Rockets' jersey."

Jay was confident he'd be picked for the team, even if he was off his game today. His rebound was usually reliable and his offence was pretty strong. He'd almost scored a three-pointer from above the key. Next time, it wouldn't be *almost*, it'd be *in*.

In the locker room, Kyung sat down beside Jay. "You said when I have questions, I can ask you." His voice was hushed.

"What?" Jay stuffed his basketball sneakers into his duffle bag and hauled out his street sneakers.

Kyung watched as Tyler, Colin, and Randall walked past them and left the locker room. Then he continued, still in a lowered voice. "Coach Willis tells us that Colin is MVP, but then he says he almost was not MVP. I do not understand."

"Colin's got attitude issues. That's no secret. It's mostly ego, but he's got a temper, too. Like Coach said."

"But he was MVP."

"Mostly, Colin fakes not having attitude issues. And mostly, it works."

"Coach Willis watches him very closely."

"Coach doesn't miss a thing."

Kyung put on his jacket and zipped it, turning the collar up at the back. "And I see you are trying to avoid Colin. When you play in drills with him, you make more mistakes."

"What're you talking about?" Jay's tone was harsh.

"I will mind my own business," Kyung said calmly.

"I didn't mean that the way it sounded. Sorry. It's just —"

"I will mind my own business," Kyung repeated. He picked up his backpack and left the locker room.

Jay looked at the closed door, still holding one sneaker in his hand. Though he'd been trying to ignore it, the problem wasn't going away. Colin might have been his best friend last year, clowning around at practices and teaming with him to make plays work. But he wasn't his friend anymore.

It was weird to think that the obstacle getting in the way of that championship banner might not be the other basketball teams at all. It might be right here on his own team.

He tied his sneakers quickly. Kyung would probably still be waiting for his ride home. It was time to come clean and let him know what was up. Jay's temporary move to Centreville. Playing for the Cougars. Everything.

"Glad you're still here," Jay said as he walked outside.

"I need to tell you about some stuff."

Kyung shifted his backpack from one shoulder to the other. He looked at Jay but wasn't smiling.

A car pulled up and a couple of guys climbed in, leaving Jay and Kyung standing alone under the bright spotlight above the main entrance.

"Mostly it's stuff that happened a while ago, but it'll clear up a few things about what's going on right now."

"I should not have so many questions," said Kyung.

"I'd do the same thing if I was in a new school with a whole bunch of new people. It's just common sense you'd try to figure things out."

Kyung looked at Jay, waiting.

"Well, to start with, I was best friends with Colin since about grade six. I'd stay at his place or he'd come to mine. Stuff like that. We both made the basketball team and that was pretty great. Then he started on this ego thing. It was like anything could get him riled up, especially when basketball was involved. He was practically a different guy. Like he had to win, no matter what."

"In Korea, when a player is like Colin, he would not be MVP."

"Like I said, he's pretty good at faking."

"It will not always be so easy," said Kyung. "Soon he will have problems."

"Yeah, well, you're probably right about that."

"He is not your best friend because of poor sportsmanship?"

"Sort of. I had to move to Centreville with my family last February and live with my grandfather. We had a fire at our place."

"A fire?"

"No one was hurt or anything, but the house needed a lot of renovations. Anyway, I had to switch schools. It was still basketball season and I ended up playing some games with the Centreville Cougars. The first one was against the Rockets."

"I am definitely understanding now."

"It gets a bit more complicated." Jay took a deep breath, and then continued. "There was this girl I was going with for a while. About a week after I moved to Centreville, Colin was going with her. They're not together now, but . . ."

Kyung looked thoughtful. "These complications explain why you are off your game and why you avoid Colin."

"Right."

"This is not only a problem for Colin. It will also become a problem for you."

Jay sighed. "Right again."

3 TEAM CAPTAIN

Jay and the rest of the players got into warm-up action as soon as they entered the gym. "Focus on what's weak and make it strong," Coach Willis always said.

"Good work, David. That's the stuff. Brendan, how's the knee? Bit better? Good. What's with the lopsided posture, Cory? Square up. Square up." Coach Willis wandered around the gym, watching layups and rebounds, checking on quick chest passes, and noting the pace of guys who jogged the perimeter. "Lookin' good, guys. Lookin' good." Finally, he called everyone together. "Okay! Gimme a circle over here!"

Everyone stopped the action, caught the basketballs, and gathered around their coach.

"We've had a couple weeks of tryouts and now we're ready to move forward," Coach Willis announced. "First thing, I want to thank all of you for putting in your best efforts. Showing me your best basketball. I appreciate that. There are a lot of great basketball players for me to choose from — more than there's room for on the Rockets A team. You already know that. But I expect to see everyone in front of me right now at all our games, whether you're on the basketball court or up in the bleachers cheerin' us on."

Everyone clapped to show they were with the coach all the way.

"In the morning, I'll post the team roster outside my office. You know the routine. After school tomorrow, the Rockets will come together as a team for the first time this season. You'll be told your positions and uniforms will be handed out. Then we'll choose our team captain. From there, we start work on landing our spot at the regionals."

Jay glanced up at the championship banners. He thought about the promise he'd made to himself and pictured one of the blank spaces on the wall occupied at the end of the basketball season. The roster to be posted outside the coach's office the next morning would have only ten names on it. There were almost twenty guys sitting there on the floor with Jay. Coach Willis would use his strongest players in the starting line, but he also had to keep an eye on the future when senior guys moved on to high school. He'd need to make sure there were new players in the mix, too.

In the first practice, Tyler had been singled out for team awareness. Jay figured that Coach Willis was thinking of Tyler for point guard. A point guard was responsible for calling plays and getting the ball into the opponent's territory. It was like being the coach on the floor. But Tyler was the best rebounder and defender. No one could stop him under the basket. That might put him in number 4 position, power forward.

Colin could be picked for position 1, point guard. He had the ball-handling skills. With Colin at 1 and Tyler at 4, maybe — just maybe — Jay could be picked for 5, centre. Coach Willis might focus on Jay's shooting skills and strong defensive plays . . . and overlook his height.

★ ★ ★

A crowd was already crammed around the roster posted outside Coach Willis's office when Jay got there the next morning. He didn't need to ask guys if they made the cut or not — their faces said it all. As Brendan passed by, he said something about how he probably didn't make it because of his knee injury. Cory gave David a high-five, then walked over to Jay and buddy-punched his arm. "See you at practice!"

Jay carefully read through the whole list. Near the bottom was Kyung's name. He looked around, but Kyung was nowhere in sight.

When Jay walked into homeroom, Kyung was at his desk, double-checking his math homework.

"Hey, Kyung! Congrats on making the team!"

"What? I made the team?"

"Didn't you check the roster?"

"I . . . I did not believe Coach Willis would pick me."

"Come on. Let's go take a look. You're playing for the Richmond Rockets!"

A few guys were still standing beside the coach's bulletin board, reading the roster. Jay pointed at the name second from the bottom, *Yi, Kyung*. Kyung grinned. Then he carefully reread the list, running his finger down the page. His expression suddenly turned serious.

"What's with the downer face?" Jay asked.

"I don't know if I can play my best basketball. Not like I played in Korea."

"Don't sweat it. That's where practice comes in. It takes a while for any team to gel. And then — wham! They're there! A solid basketball team on the way to being champions!"

★ ★ ★

There was a new energy in the gym as the Richmond Rockets came out of the locker room to start their first team practice. Jay began running laps, concentrating on his posture, his breathing, the rhythm of his sneakers on the polished floor. By the end of this practice, he'd once again have his white and blue Rockets' uniform. He was aware of an invisible thread of tension in the gym — no one knew yet which position they'd be assigned.

Coach Willis stopped the warm-up and divided the new team for the first scrimmage. "Green against blue. Grab a pinny when I call your name. Greens: Tyler, Colin, Jay, Steve, and Kyung. Blues: Cory, Finn, Randall, Dave, and Mitchell."

As the guys tied on their pinnies, Coach Willis shouted out their positions. Though these weren't permanent spots, they would indicate how the coach was thinking about his new team. Everyone listened up. "Greens. Tyler, you're point guard, position 1. Kyung, I want you in position 2, shooting guard. Jay you're number 3 forward. Steve you're number 4 forward. And Colin, you're number 5, centre. Blues —"

Jay stopped listening. Position 3 — *small forward*. Lots of players who held the position weren't small, but Jay figured he was placed there more because of his height than because of his ball handling or his scoring. But at five feet, seven inches, he wasn't actually the smallest guy in the gym. He tried to remind himself that this was just a scrimmage and not the final lineup.

Colin's height had landed him at centre. Tyler did a great job as centre last season, but maybe the coach was testing new ground. Point guard was a good position for Tyler. He knew his game and could easily call the plays, especially for offence. And his attitude wasn't negative like Colin's.

Kyung tied his green pinny and adjusted the safety strap on his glasses. He looked over at Jay and smiled. He didn't seem worried about where Coach Willis placed him. He was just glad to be playing for the Rockets.

During the scrimmage, Coach Willis dissected every move: *Why did that bounce pass go wide? How many seconds was the ball blocked? Where was the receiver? Who called the play? What happened to defence? Who was under the basket for that rebound? Someone remind us where your feet should be for a left-hand shot.*

A couple of times, the coach switched up positions. Tyler and Colin traded spots and Kyung was given Steve's forward position. But not once was Jay moved. As centre position began to fade from his hopes, he tried to think positively about playing forward. When he scored a three-point basket from the right corner, he couldn't miss the look on Coach Willis's face — maybe scoring would determine his team job after all.

At the end of practice, when all the players were sitting on the floor, Coach Willis checked his notes. He jotted down something and scribbled out something else. He tapped his clipboard thoughtfully. "Well, guys, here's our starting lineup: point guard, Tyler; shooting guard, Jay; number 3 forward, Mitchell. Randall, you're number 4 forward; Colin, you're centre."

Jay looked from Coach Willis to Mitchell and back to the coach again. Didn't he mean Jay as forward and Mitchell as shooting guard?

But the coach didn't backtrack. "Finn, you're our sixth man. And the rest of you'll get lots of game action.

No one's a bench-warmer on this team."

"Uh, Coach?" said Jay. "Can I ask a question?"

"What's on your mind?"

"Well . . ." He hesitated. "Just now, you said I'd be playing in number 2 spot. Shooting guard."

"Yes."

"Well, I mean . . . I played forward all through practice and —"

"And now you're playing guard. Is there a problem with that?"

Jay took the cue from the tone of Coach Willis's voice. "No. No problem."

"Good. That's what I like to hear. Anyone else have questions?" He waited. "No one?"

"How much switching up are you planning on doing?" asked Randall.

"Depends. This isn't pro basketball. I want you guys to get experience all over the court so you can be confident no matter where you are. Bottom line: we want our best players where we need them." He looked around. "Any more questions? If not, let's move on. Steve and Finn, get the box of uniforms out of my office, please."

Coach Willis called out names and numbers, checking them off as players came forward to get their uniforms. He called Jay to pick up seventeen, his old number. At least something would stay the same.

"You guys know that last year's players were

responsible for washing those uniforms at the end of the season, making sure they were in the best condition. No put-down intended, but I recommend you wash them again."

That got a few laughs. As they picked up their jerseys, a couple of guys covered their noses as if the jerseys reeked.

"One final piece of business before we call it a day," said Coach Willis. "Team captain. Most of you guys know we follow the democratic process in choosing our team captain — nominations, secret ballot, and the guy with the most votes wins. And it's no popularity contest. Idiots can be popular. You guys know the qualities our team captain needs to have. Let's hear them. Shout them out."

"Good communicator!"

"Leads by example!"

"A people person!"

"Someone who hustles!"

"Sets a good example!"

"Somebody already said that."

"Makes the right decisions!"

"He's someone who'll listen!"

"Knows when to kid around and when to be serious!"

"All great qualities," said Coach Willis. "Anything else?"

"He isn't afraid to call guys on stuff they do wrong,"

said Randall. "On or off the court."

"That's a good reminder, Randall." The coach glanced around, making eye contact with each player. "When you walk out that gym door this afternoon, you are a member of the Richmond Rockets A basketball team. You represent us and your school, like Randall said, on and off the court. I've always held my team to that standard and I expect your team captain to do the same." He paused to let the weight of his words sink in. "Time for nominations." He set up a flip chart and scrawled *TEAM CAPTAIN* across the top of the page.

Tyler raised his hand. "I nominate Colin."

"I nominate Tyler." Colin grinned.

"Not so fast," said Coach Willis. "Colin, do you accept the nomination?"

"Sure. Why not?" He smirked as if winning the vote was a no-brainer.

The coach wrote Colin's name on the chart paper. "Tyler?"

"I'll pass. Colin's our guy for captain."

"We have a democratic process here, Tyler. That'll decide who's the guy for captain," said Coach Willis, frowning. "So let's hear some other nominations. Come on, guys. We should have three or four names here."

"Mitchell," someone called out.

"Okay with you, Mitchell?" He wrote the second name on the list when Mitchell nodded.

Kyung raised his hand. "I have a nomination." He

stood up as though he was about to make a speech. "For team captain, I nominate Jay Hirtle."

This caught Jay off guard. It wasn't just the nomination. There was something in the way Kyung spoke — so serious. He seemed absolutely sure that Jay was the best guy to lead the team to victory . . . and that Colin wasn't.

Colin was scowling at Kyung.

"What about it, Jay?" asked Coach Willis. "Do you accept?"

"Uh . . . well . . ." Jay wasn't sure he could actually do the job. First, there was the complication of being back with the Rockets after playing for the Cougars. The rest of the team might not be sure they could count on him. And then there was the complication of Colin and the problems he'd likely stir up. It wouldn't be easy being team captain.

Kyung watched Jay, not smiling, not moving.

"Yes," said Jay, finally. "I accept."

Kyung remained standing until Jay's name was written on the list.

"Any more names to add here?" Coach Willis tapped the marker against his palm. "That's it, then? Okay." He drew a line under the three names. "There's a bunch of pencils on my desk. How about getting them, Cory? David, tear this paper into ballots and give one to each player. And remember, this vote's secret. Talk about it all you want later, but right now, make your own decision and write it on your ballot."

When the votes were collected, Coach Willis took them into his office and closed the door.

Kyung sat beside Jay. "Guess who I voted for," he joked.

"Thanks," said Jay. "For the nomination, too. I wasn't expecting that."

"You are fair. You communicate. You listen."

Coach Willis came out of his office. "Okay, guys. It's a close race here but we have a decision. I'm not giving out numbers because numbers don't matter. Mitchell, Jay, and Colin — thank you for stepping forward to run for team captain. A nomination is an achievement. Congratulations to all three of you."

Everyone applauded.

"And now, the guy who'll push you to do your best, who'll hear you out when times are tough, who'll set a good — no, scratch that — who'll set a *great* example both on and off the court. Your new team captain for the Richmond Rockets is . . . Jay Hirtle!"

4 ON AND OFF THE COURT

"Go tell your grandfather your news about being team captain, Jay," said his dad as they arrived at Gramp's. "He's probably over on Moyle's wharf."

"I'm going, too!" said Sam. "And Rudy!"

"Put him on his leash, then."

From the lane leading down the hill to the wharf, they could see Gramp stacking lobster traps on the edge of the wharf beside Moyle's Cape Island boat. The two fishermen had been neighbours all their lives, though Gramp was older than Moyle and was now retired from fishing.

Moyle's only son, Simon, came out of the fish store where all the gear was kept — barrels for bait, coiled ropes hanging on hooks beside jiggers and gaffs, bright yellow waterproofed coats and pants, large rubber boots.

"Hi, Jay. Sam. Hey, Rudy, how's it goin' fella?" Simon bent down to give Rudy a strong rub behind his ears and along his thick neck. "There's a good dog."

"Not long till lobster season," said Jay.

"Lots to do before then. Of course, nothing'll stop your grandfather from helping out. Misses the work, for sure. And having his own boat. We'll get him out there on the water with us, one of these calm days."

"Oil calm days," said Sam.

Simon laughed. "You're sounding just like your grandfather."

They walked out to the end of the wharf, Rudy tugging on his leash the whole way.

"Looks like we got some reinforcements comin' to help out," said Gramp as he put another lobster trap in place.

Moyle stepped up from the boat and onto the wharf.

"Jay's got something super, super big to tell, Gramp!" said Sam.

"Oh?"

"Don't exaggerate, Sam. It's no big deal."

They all looked at Jay, waiting.

"It's . . . well, it's just about being captain. For our basketball team."

"They voted, and Jay won captain!" If Sam had had a megaphone, his cheering couldn't have been louder.

"Now that's awful good news," said Gramp. "Captain. Well, well."

"Congratulations there, son," Moyle said.

"Very important job," said Simon. "Just like being a captain of one of these boats."

"Lotta responsibility," said Gramp, nodding seriously.

Jay looked down at the weathered boards of the wharf. *Responsibility* wasn't something he needed to be reminded about. Since yesterday's vote, that word kept floating up into his mind and clouding him with doubts.

"But don't go fallin' in love with the sound of your own voice barking out orders," Moyle said.

"Oh, now, look who's talking," said Simon. "Dad's got more bark than that dog has. I'm telling you guys, you haven't been out on the water with this one here. It only gets quiet when he takes a nap, and that doesn't last longer than ten minutes."

"Try to teach my son everything I know about this business, and look at the thanks I get," said Moyle. "One thing I'll tell you about being captain, whether it's a boat captain or a basketball captain — it's not going to be what you say or what you do that'll cause trouble. It'll be someone else's idea about what you say or do."

"Now that's the truth, sure as I'm standing here," said Gramp.

Jay picked up a short piece of braided twine, bright turquoise and frayed at the end. He spun it between his thumb and finger, watching the unravelled strands whirl. It didn't take too much imagination to see how the chunk of twine was like a warning to him as team captain. If he wasn't careful, his team could unravel and things would just spin out of control.

"When you're ready to bark out some orders, Captain

Dad, let's get some more work accomplished before those clouds open up and dump rain down on us."

"I'll go on over to the house," said Gramp. "You're almost done for the day. See you tomorrow."

"Thanks for the hand," said Moyle.

Sam and Rudy ran ahead, but Jay kept a slower pace with his grandfather as they made their way back up the lane.

"Captain, eh?" Gramp said. "If the boys on your team gave you their votes, then looks like they agree with my opinion about the kind of captain you'll be."

"It was a close vote."

"Still and all, you're the team captain now and there's no changing that."

On the drive home, Jay's thoughts went back to the conversations about boat captains and team captains. He still had the braided twine in his hand.

"What's that bit of old twine, Jay?" asked his father.

"Lemme see," said Sam from the back seat.

Rudy pushed his head forward in the off chance they were talking about something good to eat.

"It's nothing, Sam," said Jay. "Just a frayed end cut off some lobster gear."

Sam and Rudy settled into the back seat again. Rudy flopped down with an exaggerated sigh and Sam began to count red cars that passed. "First red car!"

"Gramp's pretty proud of you being voted team captain," said his father. "It was written all over his face."

"Yeah." Jay spun the frayed twine.

"Not sure you're actually keen about the job, though. Something up?"

"Not really."

"It'll take some getting used to."

"Yeah, I guess."

"This is an honour your teammates have given you. They wouldn't've done that if they didn't think you were the right man for the job. And I know you've got what it takes to be the best team captain there is."

"Thanks, Dad." Jay stuffed the braided twine into his jacket pocket.

"Two!" yelled Sam.

"Do parked cars count? There's a red car in that gas station," said their dad.

"Three!"

Jay looked out the window at the skeleton branches of bare maple trees.

★ ★ ★

"Check this out," said Kyung, scrolling through the photos on his cell. "Wait, not that one. Not that one. This one. Look, this is my friend in Korea. We have been friends for a long time."

A guy wearing a red team jersey was standing in a gym, a basketball tucked under his arm. His thick black hair was cut short on the sides with longer hair falling across his forehead, a lot like Kyung's. In the background were other players in red jerseys and a few in white.

"His name is Min Ki. His school is Whimoon High School in Seoul. His team has won the basketball championship many times."

"Is that the school you went to?" asked Jay.

"Min Ki lives near my parents' house, but we did not go to the same school."

The bell rang and they started toward homeroom.

"Hey! Watch where you're going!"

Jay heard the shout and felt the pain in his arm at the same time. He caught his balance and rubbed his arm where Colin's elbow had just planted a bruise.

"What's with crowding me?" said Colin, his voice still raised.

"What're you talking about? You just slammed my arm," Jay said.

"You were crowding me. Tyler saw the whole thing. He'll back me up."

Tyler looked around sheepishly and said nothing. A few people had stopped to see what was going on.

"We are Rockets," said Kyung, his voice quiet and cautious. "On and off the court."

"Jay crossed over to the Cougars' side," said Colin. "And the way I see it, he never came back. But you probably don't know anything about that or you wouldn't have set him up for team captain."

"Is that what this is all about? Me being team captain?"

"Team captain's nothing," said Colin. "It's a joke."

"Team captain is not a joke," said Kyung. "It is serious. A team captain has many responsibilities and many good qualities. That is why Jay was chosen for the position."

"Oh, so I don't have what it takes to be captain?"

"He's not saying that," said Jay. "What's with you, anyway?"

"Come on, Colin," said Tyler. "Let's just get going."

Jay watched them walk away. The stream of people in the hall divided and moved around him and Kyung as if they were boulders.

"This will become a problem for the Rockets," said Kyung.

"Tell me about it."

"Colin is holding a grudge. I think it is for two reasons. One, because you are team captain and he would like the position. Two, because you play for the Cougars and they are the regional champions."

"*Played*. Past tense. Not *play*."

"Yes. Past tense. This is what I mean. But for Colin, last year is the same as the present. He is not forgetting."

If the situation was different, Jay could ignore Colin. Just stay outside his space. But they were Rockets and Jay was team captain. *On and off the court*, like Kyung said. Jay needed to defuse the Colin bomb before things got any closer to the detonation point. The question was, how could he do that?

At lunch break, Jay headed to the gym. As he came down the stairs, he noticed Brendan sitting under the stairwell with a few friends. One was playing a guitar.

"Hey, Brendan," Jay said. "Wanna shoot a few baskets?"

"You mean now?"

"Sure. Why not?"

Brendan stood up, rubbed his knee, then caught up to Jay.

"What's with hanging out under the stairwell?" asked Jay. "You always shoot baskets at lunch. You have your game to think about."

"I didn't make the team."

"So?"

"So why practise shooting baskets?"

"Coach Willis isn't playing you because your knee injury needs time to heal. But you still have to stay with the game. Coach wants you strong for next year."

"You think so?"

"He has to plan for the future even while he's concentrating on the present. You'll be on the team next year when your knee's ready for more basketball action."

There was a pickup game on one side of the gym, guys and girls playing together. With them were Colin and Tyler.

"Let's grab a basketball," said Jay, heading to the

other side of the gym. "You stand on the free-throw line and I'll feed you the ball."

Out of five shots, Brendan was on the mark with three.

"Okay, now go back to the three-point line," said Jay.

After he'd shot five more from just behind the three-point line, Brendan tossed the ball to Jay. "Let's switch up."

"Take it easy on rebounds, though. Watch that knee."

A few shouts came from the pickup game. The action had stopped. Tyler was holding the ball and it was obvious that the girl standing in front of him thought she should have it. Colin's opinion on the out-of-bounds ruling was loud and clear.

"Someone should tell Colin pickup basketball's supposed to be fun," said Brendan.

Jay decided not to say anything about Colin's competitive streak. But again, he found himself picturing a bomb waiting to explode. He turned and made his shot from the free-throw line. The ball swished through the net and bounced before Brendan even saw it leave Jay's hands.

"Hey," said Jay, "I got an idea for how you could stay connected to the team. Why not ask Coach Willis if you can be team manager? Look, he just went in his office. Might be a good time right now."

As Brendan knocked on the coach's office door, Jay left the gym. He was pretty sure Coach Willis would take Brendan on as team manager. It gave him a good feeling, like he'd done something right as team captain. Something his dad and Gramp would both be proud of.

Jay found Kyung waiting for him by his locker. "I have been thinking," said Kyung, "and I may have a very good idea to end this trouble with Colin."

"I'm listening." Jay sorted through his books to find what he needed for afternoon classes — French and math.

"Tyler is the person you must talk to."

"Tyler?"

"He is Colin's friend. He could help."

"Why should he?"

"Because he is on the Rockets team." Kyung looked very sure of himself. "Let's go to find him now."

"I saw him in the gym playing pickup. But Colin's there too. How's that gonna work?"

Kyung started toward the gym and Jay followed. He wasn't the least bit sure this idea was a good one.

The pickup game had already ended and Tyler was nowhere in sight. Neither was Colin.

"So much for that," said Jay, relieved. A confrontation with Colin wasn't what he needed. "Guess we'll just have to see how things go. Maybe we're over-reacting, anyway."

Kyung took out his cell phone and texted a quick message. An answer came right back. "Finn says Tyler is on his way upstairs. He is by himself."

Again, Jay followed Kyung.

"There he is," said Kyung when he spotted Tyler. "I will wait downstairs. You must talk to him by yourself, one-on-one."

Jay stepped toward Tyler. "Uh, got a minute?"

Tyler looked surprised. "Sure."

"What was going on there in the hall? You know, with Colin slamming my arm and being so riled up? I don't get it."

"Yeah, well, Colin gets ticked off. It doesn't take much."

"He slammed into me on purpose. You were there."

"I was just walking along, and all of a sudden, there's this thing happening. I didn't see anything."

"Look, if Colin gets ticked off at me or anyone else on our team, it's my problem. No matter where we are. I have to make sure there's no inside conflict that'll mess things up for the whole team."

"What am I supposed to do about it? Colin does what he wants, and nothing I say's gonna change him. You're the captain. You talk to him." Tyler started to walk away. "It's my team, too, you know. I don't want things messed up either."

When Jay got to the bottom of the stairs, Kyung was waiting.

"Tyler told me to talk to Colin. As if the guy'd listen."

"In-fighting is big trouble for the Rockets," said Kyung.

"Unless I can do something about it."

5 DEFENCE AND AGGRESSION

"Okay, guys. Listen up," said Coach Willis. "I want to introduce your team manager. Come over here, Brendan."

Brendan got up from the floor and stood beside Coach Willis.

"This guy came to see me the other day and volunteered for the position of team manager. Told me he wants to stay connected to the team while his knee injury heals up. Right away, I told him yes. Why? Because Brendan's the kind of player I want. When he doesn't make the team, he figures out how to stay with the game. I admire that. Any coach'd admire that."

Jay gave Brendan a thumbs-up.

"As team manager, Brendan will keep us organized: basketballs, uniforms, water bottles. He'll keep stats on assists, points, turnovers, and so on. He'll help get practices set up and keep attendance records. He'll be the guy you call if you can't make a practice. And you already know that something better be broken if you say you're gonna miss a practice."

A few guys chuckled, though most of them knew Coach Willis was pretty serious. Missing a practice was at the very top of his *DO NOT DO* list. Missing two practices without an excuse was an automatic suspension for the next game.

"If Brendan is in charge of all that stuff, what's the team captain supposed to be doing?"

Jay didn't need to turn around to know who had spoken. And from the sarcastic tone in Colin's voice, more trouble was on the way.

"Well, Colin," said the coach, "with all your basketball experience, I'm surprised you're unable to distinguish between team captain and team manager. Anyone else confused about those jobs?" He looked around and got no reply, just as he expected. "Right. So I suggest you take a little break, Colin, and do some research in the library." He looked at his watch. "Come back in ten minutes and give us a little summary about the basic jobs of team manager and team captain."

Colin didn't move. "I was only joking around."

"I wasn't," said Coach Willis firmly.

Colin hesitated, but then got up and slowly left the gym, all eyes on him.

"Okay, that's enough distraction for today," said Coach Willis. "Let's get some practice in, guys! Jay, talk us through some defence drills. Everyone form a line and listen up."

Jay's brain suddenly went on pause. No ideas, no

words, no images filled the empty space. "Defence," he muttered to himself.

Everyone waited for him to speak.

Then he said out loud, "Defence!" He didn't have a clue what he would say next, but he kept going anyway. "There's one basic word for defence and that word is *aggression*. Defence is about aggression. If there's no aggression, the offensive player can do whatever he wants."

Coach Willis was smiling.

Jay could feel himself getting into it. "Randall, you're defence. Show us the basics for keeping your balance and effective blocking."

When Randall had finished his demonstration, Jay pointed to Steve. "Steve, you're offence. Let's see Randall's defence in action. When I say *change*, you guys'll switch."

A few minutes later, Coach Willis blew the whistle and the action stopped. Colin had returned to the gym, a piece of paper in his hand.

"Let's see what you have there," said Coach Willis. He glanced down Colin's research notes. "Hmm." Then he folded the paper and put it into his pocket. "I won't take up practice time with a lesson about what a team manager does and what a team captain does, since these guys already know the difference. And now, you also know the difference, according to this paper. So get yourself into these drills and listen to your team captain."

Jay avoided looking at Colin. The most important

thing was to keep the practice from going off the rails. "Okay, everyone. Pair up and grab a ball. Go over the defensive player's hand positions for wherever the offensive player has the ball. Take turns on defence and offence."

Kyung picked up a basketball and stood in front of Jay, holding the ball as if he was about to make an overhead pass.

Jay took the challenge. He put his hand under the ball and quickly lifted up. Kyung lost possession.

"Very good move," said Kyung.

For the last thirty minutes of practice, Coach Willis called for three-on-three games. He would referee on one half of the court and Brendan on the other. When the numbering off was finished and the teams were formed, Jay knew he was in for a challenge. He would be playing on the same team as Colin.

"We don't just want cuts to the basket for layup shots," said Coach Willis. "You have lots of options. Use your high post. Look for your player at the elbow of the key and feed him the ball. He can slow things down, pass forward, or even go for the shot. And remember, Brendan, don't call free throws till we're down to crunch time — that's three-on-three rules. Okay, let's see some Rockets' basketball!" He grabbed a ball and went to the other end of the gym.

Jay already had a plan to make the three-on-three work: focus on the basketball at all times and avoid eye contact with Colin.

Brendan flipped a coin and the other team got first possession.

Within seconds, they scored.

"Two–zero," said Brendan. "Take it back."

Jay bounce-passed to Randall as Colin picked a spot under the basket. The ball came back to Jay and he made a long shot from the top of the key. It hit the backboard and they lost possession.

Colin was miffed. "Keep your head up, Randall. I was wide open. You should've passed to me."

"You were blocked."

"Get glasses."

Jay kept his focus on the basketball. When his opponent held the ball above his head, Jay slipped his hand under it and quickly tipped it up. He caught the ball and pivoted. Colin was cutting toward the basket and Jay made a snap pass. Colin fumbled. The ball rolled out of bounds.

Brendan blew his whistle.

Jay was sure his pass had been right on the mark. Colin's fumble had to be on purpose.

Randall's defence kept the ball out of action while Jay blocked his guard's path to the top of the key. The player took a chance and tried a shot over Randall's head. It went wide. Colin got the rebound and made the jump for two points.

"Two–two," said Brendan.

When the score was 14–10 for the other team, Jay

took a risk and jogged close to Colin as they got into position. "Rebound," he said. It would be the surest way they could close up the score.

Colin shrugged.

Randall passed from behind the arc and Jay had the ball. Defence fell for Randall's fake toward the basket. Jay went up for the long shot. It rebounded just as Colin freed himself from his guard. He grabbed the ball. As he jumped, his guard jumped, too, hitting Colin's arm.

"It's a foul," said Brendan. "Take it back."

"What're you talking about? We get the free throw," said Colin.

"Only if the score's 14–14," said Brendan. "That's what Coach said."

"That's nuts!"

"Let's just play," said Jay.

"No one's asking you."

"Come on," said Randall. "It's only practice. It doesn't matter."

"You think like that," said Colin, "and guess what? When it's a real game, you'll still think it doesn't matter." He picked up the basketball and walked past the top of the key to start the action again.

His chest pass to Jay was sloppy. Jay fumbled and the other team grabbed the ball. In one quick pick-and-go, they scored. 16–10.

"Game!"

When the action at the other end of the gym

stopped, the coach called the players together. "Couple more practices before we face MacLeod," he said. "Hope those guys'll be ready for us because we're ready for them. Am I right?"

Everyone cheered and a few players gave each other high-fives.

"And I guess I don't need to remind you that we're in charge of running things at the dance tonight. Everyone knows what they signed up for. Remember to wear your jerseys over your clothes. Keep a high profile. Rockets get half the take at the door and the canteen, so I'm expecting all of you to do the work and show our gratitude."

After practice, Jay helped Brendan stack the balls on the racks in the storage room.

"I know what Colin was doing out there," said Brendan. "He was trying to make you look bad. No one could've caught that last pass."

"He's just in a bad mood. He'll get over it." Jay knew this really wasn't true.

"You should say something to Coach Willis."

"It'd probably make it worse. Let's see how things work out."

"It's your call."

"How what works out?" Coach Willis walked into the storage room, his clipboard in his hand.

"Uh, nothing, Coach," said Jay.

"Looks pretty serious for nothing."

A couple of seconds of silence filled the gap before Coach Willis spoke again. "Right. I get the picture. It's something for the captain and the manager to sort out. I'm okay with that. But whatever this is, don't wait until it's too late before you fill me in."

"For sure, Coach," said Jay.

Coach Willis handed the clipboard to Brendan. "I need you to count basketballs. I have two columns here — one for balls that're okay for practice and one for the game balls. If any are in bad shape, put them in my office."

"I'll give him a hand," said Jay.

When Coach Willis left the storage room and was safely out of earshot, Jay said, "Thanks for not saying anything about Colin."

"Just doing what you asked me to." Brendan picked up a soft basketball and checked the seams. He tossed it on the floor.

Jay picked up a blue and white game ball, gave it a thorough check, and put it back on the shelf.

When the count was finished and Brendan had locked the storage room, he turned to Jay. "What'd you sign up for at the dance?"

"Clean-up."

"I'm on tickets. I gotta be there early."

"Most guys'll go early. Keep a high profile, like Coach says."

★ ★ ★

Everyone who lived far from the school depended on getting a drive to dances, usually from parents but sometimes from older sisters or brothers. Cars pulled into the driveway that curved in front of the school's main entrance, and three or four people spilled out of each one. Jay's mother dropped off Jay and Kyung on her way to evening rounds at the hospital.

Mr. Haley was beside the ticket table, greeting everyone and teasing whoever he could. Two girls dressed the same — pink tops, black skirts, black shoes — were in front of Jay and Kyung, getting their tickets. "Do you ladies go to this school? I don't remember registering twins this year." Then he tossed a smile at Kyung. "Ready to teach us some Korean dance moves, Kyung?"

"It is the same as Canadian dancing, sir. Not complicated."

The gym was soon packed with people dancing, some with partners but most just joining the crowd, doing their own thing. Music blasted out from two huge speakers and lights flashed colour on the dancers. The DJ checked his playlist and took requests from the groupies in front of the stage.

Everyone seemed up for partying. Kyung crammed himself inside the mass of dancers and was soon lost in the blast and beat of the music. His fists jabbed the air above his head, his black and orange hair tossing wildly with every unpredictable move he made.

But Jay wasn't really in the party mood. The stuff that had happened that day still messed up his brain. He stood in a shadow at the side of the gym, listening and watching.

After a while, he headed to the canteen. Behind the counter was Coach Willis . . . and Colin. Quite a few people were waiting to be served. Jay tried to stay on the side closest to Coach Willis, but that didn't work. When his turn came, the coach was leaning into the fridge, clanging through cans of pop to find what someone had asked for.

Colin served the person next to Jay before he finally turned to him. "Yeah?"

"I'll take a ginger ale and chips, plain. Please." He tried to keep his voice neutral.

Colin put the pop and chips on the counter and picked up Jay's change.

Suddenly, an odd feeling washed over Jay. It wasn't worry, anger, or even frustration. It was the kind of calm that comes when all of a sudden, you realize something is true. No blurred lines. *Why should this guy keep on being such a jerk and get away with it like no one sees what's going on?* "Whatever's bugging you, you need to get over it," Jay said.

"What're you talking about?" said Colin, angrily.

"Stop trying to mess things up for the Rockets."

"I'm not trying to mess things up!" Colin's voice had raised a few more decibels and people around them were beginning to stare. "You're the one hoping the Rockets will lose to your Cougars."

Coach Willis put two cans of pop down on the counter. "Gentlemen, we need to have a conversation. Be in Mr. Haley's office in five minutes. Jay, find Randall and David and ask them to take over canteen duty."

When they met in the principal's office, Coach Willis shut the door quietly behind them and pulled three chairs together. "Now, it's not like I don't have a pretty good idea what's going on here. But I'll give you both a chance to talk and all of us will listen. No interruptions. Who wants to start?"

Jay looked down at his hands.

Colin was silent.

Coach Willis waited a couple of seconds, then spoke. "Okay. If you guys don't want to talk, I will. This is not a good situation. Here I have my team captain and the guy who's our MVP. Instead of two players setting the bar right up there as a model for everyone else on our team, what've I got? Two guys acting like tomcats in an alley." He stood up. "Tell you what. I'm going to leave you here a while by yourselves. You can work this out, or you can just sit here saying nothing. That's up to you. But until I come back into this office, you're going nowhere. Bottom line is, if you guys can't get past this personal conflict, then you can't do your best job for the Rockets. I have the rest of my team to think about."

When the door closed, Colin leaned forward with

his elbows on his knees, still silent. Jay rubbed his hand across his mouth, then leaned back and closed his eyes. They could hear the blast and thud of music coming from the gym.

Jay thought of Kyung dancing, oblivious to everyone around him, having a great time. Right now, he envied that guy .

A few minutes went by. Colin shifted in his chair and cleared his throat. He blew a gust of air from his mouth. Still he said nothing.

Jay heaved a sigh and looked around the office. On the wall above Mr. Haley's desk was a huge poster of a golf course with the sun coming up, or maybe going down, through trees at the top of a hill. He studied every detail — the pond in the foreground, the greens, the sand traps shaped like kidney beans, the golf cart going along a dirt trail, a couple of guys standing around waiting for the guy in the middle to make a put shot. Maybe Mr. Haley golfed there. Everyone knew he was nuts about golf so —

Colin got up and walked out.

When Coach Willis came back into the office, he asked the obvious question. "Where's Colin?"

"I don't know. He just walked out a couple minutes ago."

"Did you guys talk?"

"No."

"I'm not surprised. But I am disappointed." The coach didn't sit down. "You're the captain, Jay. I expected you to take the ball and run with it. There's tension between you and Colin. Am I wrong?"

"No. I don't know. Maybe it won't turn into anything." Jay wasn't even convincing himself. "Colin's been like this ever since I played those games for Centreville. He's calling me a traitor. That's crazy."

"And now that you're team captain, the tension's turned up a notch."

"Yeah, seems like."

"Well, right now, I got a bone to pick with Colin because of leaving this room when I told him to stay until I got back. As team captain, you need to know that if Colin can't get control of his negative attitude, he's at risk of being cut from the team. This situation is threatening to drain our competitive energy. We might need Colin's basketball talent, but not more than we need a cohesive team."

★ ★ ★

When the DJ had packed up and left, and everyone on clean-up had transformed the gym back to normal, Jay switched off the lights. Instead of clanging the large doors shut, he stood in the hall looking through the darkness, past the slice of light spilling into the gym. He walked to the end of the triangle of light and kept going until he was standing at the centre of the basketball court. Dark and deserted, the gym wasn't at all like it was in the daytime — the place where he had learned to play basketball, where he had sweated through all those practices, and where he had showed Coach Willis that he was team material.

Now he was team captain.

He pictured the Rockets there with him, wearing their blue and white jerseys, tuned into the game. Passing the ball swiftly up the floor, getting into position, setting up the play under the basket, then scoring before the opposition knew what was happening. A buzzer ending a championship game. High-fives all around.

"Is that you in there, Jay?" Kyung's voice interrupted the silence.

"Yeah."

"Are you okay?"

"Sure, I'm okay. Just doing some thinking." Jay walked toward Kyung and into the light.

"Your mother will soon come to get us. We should go outside to wait."

"Right." He closed the gym doors.

If Colin can't get control of his negative attitude, he's at risk of being cut from the team. That warning was more than just information passed along, coach to captain. Coach Willis was telling Jay that if he had a way to prevent the cut from happening, he'd better move fast. Maybe Coach Willis was willing to cut their MVP and risk losing the championship, but Jay wasn't.

6 DOWNSIZED ROCKETS

Jay woke Saturday morning to the sound of Rudy barking in the yard and Sam shouting, "No barking!" even though shouting never worked if the neighbour's cat was involved. Jay got out of bed and looked outside. There was the black cat, stepping slowly along the fence, ignoring the barking dog just a leap away.

Eventually, the cat jumped down into its own yard.

Eventually, Rudy stopped barking.

Jay grabbed his jeans off the floor and hauled them on. He wanted to make a call before breakfast. It was something he'd been thinking about since last night. "Hey, Kyung. It's me. Jay. You want to go to Centreville Monday morning? It's the start of lobster season, and we go every year to watch the boats leave the cove — Dad, me, Sam, and Mom, and Gramp, my grandfather. We'd have to pick you up by six because the boats leave at seven sharp. What do you think?"

"I think yes!"

Jay changed into his running gear and headed to

Veterans Memorial Park a few of blocks away. At least a couple times a week, he ran there, working on endurance and speed. The dirt paths through the wooded park were great for running — no sneakers slamming against pavement, no chance of ending up with an injury.

As he passed the duck pond, he thought about how Colin used to jog in that same park with him when they were trying out for the basketball team in grade seven. Colin was almost always way ahead, yelling, "Come on! Run like you mean it." Sometimes, after the run, he'd encourage Jay by saying things like "Speed's not everything. Your ball handling'll land you on the team."

It was almost impossible for Jay to picture Colin like that now. *He sees basketball more like a war zone. Enemies and allies. Losers and winners*, thought Jay. And Colin had to be a winner. Losing the team captain vote was a bigger deal for Colin than for most guys. But holding a grudge against Jay didn't make sense.

When he got back to the duck pond, Jay glanced at his watch to check his timing. He was slow, probably because he wasn't concentrating enough on running.

* * *

The streets of Richmond were quiet and dark as Jay's family arrived to pick up Kyung, who was waiting on the lighted porch. As soon as he was crammed into the back seat with Jay and Sam, introductions were made all around.

"Now you know my whole family. Except for Gramp."

"And Rudy," said Sam.

"Our dog," explained Jay.

"Rudy loves peanut butter sandwiches," Sam announced. "And sleeping on my bed. And reading with Mom."

"And barking at cats or squirrels or anything else on four legs," said Jay.

"Cows and horses and oxes and zebras and lions and giraffes and —"

Jay grabbed Sam's hat and pretended to throw it out the window.

"*Home of the Cougars.*" Kyung read the sign beneath the spotlight as they drove past Centreville School. "This is the school you played basketball for last year."

"Yeah."

"You told me the Cougars won the basketball championship."

"Third year in a row," said Jay.

"This year, the Cougars will not win."

"You got that right."

A bright light flooded Moyle's wharf, and all around the cove other lights shone on other wharves where boats were tied up, waiting for the darkness to fade. A few boats already had their engines started, but no one could untie the ropes until seven o'clock.

Gramp was standing near the end of the wharf, both hands stuffed into the pockets of his thick plaid jacket. He turned with a smile as they approached him.

"This is my grandfather," said Jay. "Gramp, this is Kyung. He's in my class and he's on my basketball team."

"Pleased to meet you, son," said Gramp, and he shook Kyung's hand.

"I am pleased to meet you, sir," said Kyung.

Though the sun had not yet come up, the sky would soon begin to fill with a pale light. A few family members and friends gathered at each wharf to wish the fishermen well on their first day of the season. Lobster traps were stacked high at the backs of all the Cape Island boats, the brightly painted buoys contrasting with the dull green of the wire traps.

Kyung snapped photos of just about everything he saw. "What are those blue and white objects?" he asked, leaning in for a closer look at Moyle's traps.

"Buoys," said Sam. "B-U-O-Y-S."

"Sam's fixated on vocabulary," said Jay. "But sometimes he actually knows what he's talking about."

"They float," said Sam. "And a rope ties the buoy to a lobster trap so you know where the trap is when it sinks to the bottom of the ocean. And everyone has different colours so no one gets mixed up."

"Take Moyle, here," added Gramp. "His are white and blue, but Peter over there's got his buoys painted orange and yellow. They can fish right alongside each other and know who owns what traps."

"Hey, Kyung," said Jay. "Check it out. Moyle's buoys are Rockets' colours — white and blue."

"So all these fishing boats are like teams with team colours. And they have captains, also," Kyung added with a grin.

But I bet boat captains don't have the same hassles as team captains, thought Jay.

"Soon time to get out there on the water," said Gramp. He went to the edge of the wharf, climbed down the wooden ladder, and stepped into the boat beside Moyle and Simon. They talked for a few minutes and had a chuckle about something. Gramp shook Moyle's hand and then Simon's before he climbed back up the ladder to stand on the wharf.

At exactly seven o'clock, as if a gun had fired to start a race, boats were untied and rumbled away from the wharves. Pointing toward the open sea, their lights beamed into the pre-dawn darkness. The smell of diesel fuel wafted across the cove. People waved and shouted their good wishes above the noise of the engines. When the boats had rounded the headland and were out of sight, people slowly walked away from the wharves.

There was no wind. The weather forecast called for only the lightest breeze during the morning and afternoon. It would be a safe first day for the fishermen and their boats.

"Do the fishing boats leave at this time every day?" asked Kyung.

"They have to wait until seven o'clock only on this first day," said Gramp. "Tomorrow, there'll be lotsa boats out there even before five. When you see their lights, you think they're stars fallen to the horizon."

Jay knew his grandfather would love to be out there on a Cape Islander, no matter what the weather and no matter what the time of day. But things had changed. Gramp no longer had his own boat or his own buoys marked with his own colours. It reminded Jay of what happened when he couldn't play basketball for the Rockets. Maybe what his grandfather was feeling was a lot like Jay had felt then. On the sidelines. Out of bounds.

"Jay Hirtle! How's it going?" Walking toward him was Mike Murphy.

"Kinda figured I'd see you around here today," said Jay. "Mike, this is Kyung. Kyung, this is Mike. He's team captain for the Centreville Cougars."

"Jay has told me about playing for your team last year," said Kyung. "Now he is the captain of the Rockets."

"Way to go, Jay! Guess you and me'll be in for some good competition this year. How's your team looking?"

"The best!" he said enthusiastically, trying to cover how he really felt. Why let his main opponent in on what was going on?

"The Rockets will win the championship this year," said Kyung.

"Gotta play to win," said Mike. "That's the name of the game. When do we play you guys, anyway?"

"Our first game's against MacLeod this Thursday. Then it's Centreville next week, I think."

"That seems right. I'll check the schedule. Guess we'll soon see who's on top when the game buzzer goes." Mike grinned. "Well, better catch my ride home. Great to see you guys."

"See ya, Mike."

"I think Mike has what it takes to be a very good team captain," said Kyung as they walked back to the car. "He has confidence in his team. Also he is very friendly about competition."

"He's a great guy," admitted Jay. "Probably the only good thing about playing basketball for the Cougars last year was getting to know Mike Murphy."

When Jay and Kyung were dropped off at school, it was still very early. Only one bus had arrived, and there were just a few cars in the teachers' parking lot.

They were walking past the main office when Mr. Haley came out into the hall.

"Jay Hirtle, just the person I need to see. Come into my office, please." Though the principal's voice was calm, there was an edge of tension that was hard to miss. Something was definitely wrong.

"I'll see you in homeroom," Jay said to Kyung as he

entered the principal's office.

"Please sit down." Mr. Haley closed his office door. "I'm placing a call to Mr. Willis. Better that you hear this from him." He punched in the numbers, then handed the phone to Jay.

"Coach? It's Jay. I'm in Mr. Haley's office."

"Jay, I have some news. You're team captain and so you need to know. I took a fall. Damn foolish thing — slipped on wet grass taking a short cut to my neighbour's. Anyway, I'm sitting here with my leg wrapped up and doctors are telling me I'm going nowhere for a while."

"Gee, Coach. I'm really sorry. I —"

"No broken bones but the ligaments are pulled. Worse than a damn break if you ask me. Painful as hell — pardon my French."

"What about our first game at MacLeod? Will you be back by then?"

"Not likely. So I'm asking you to handle things for a day or so until we get a few matters worked out."

"Handle things? Like what?"

"For starters, I'll get you to run practice after school today. Mr. Haley'll drop by and make sure things're going okay, but he'll be busy trying to find a sub who knows one end of a gym from the other and at least owns a pair of sneakers."

"Who'll be coaching us?"

"I asked Ms. Himmelman to help out and she's up for that. She can't be there for today's practice, but she'll be there for the next one. And she's going to MacLeod with her girls' team, so that's covered in case I'm not back by then. Anyway, Thursday's a long way off. Let's take it one day at a time."

"Sure, Coach. Okay. Bye."

"That injury could have been worse," said Mr. Haley as he put the phone back in place. "He might have required surgery. And then who knows how long he would've had to stay home and recuperate. He's lucky — not that he'd agree if he heard me say that. Anyway, you and Ms. Himmelman will do just fine keeping things going until he gets back. I'm sure of that."

Jay glanced out the window. A bus pulled up in front of the school and stopped behind two others. People were getting off the buses like it was just another ordinary day.

"Is there something you're particularly concerned about, Jay?"

"Uh, no, sir. There's nothing, really."

Before the bell rang to begin first class, Jay had just enough time to tell Kyung what was going on.

"This is a very challenging situation," said Kyung. Then, after a couple of seconds, he added, "My father explains that there is no learning in your life if there are no conflicts."

Jay rolled his eyes, resisting the urge to say what he felt like saying.

★ ★ ★

"So that's all I know about Coach Willis's situation for now," said Mr. Haley. "I don't need to tell you guys that he's anxious to be back here with you. And I'm sure he'll do everything in his power to make that happen. Meanwhile, Ms. Himmelman has agreed to act as your coach. She'll help you out in your next practice and, if Coach Willis can't return to school by Thursday, she'll continue on as coach for your first game of the season. All you guys have to do is put your best into your practices and then start the season with a win over MacLeod. I know you can do it!"

Jay watched Mr. Haley leave the gym. For a split second, he imagined turning away from the team and following the principal right out the gym door.

"This is useless," said Colin. "How're we supposed to practise with no coach?"

"Well . . ." Jay cleared his throat, looking past Colin to find friendly faces. "It's just for today."

"What a waste of time! I'm not staying if there's no coach. Come on, Tyler. Let's go." Colin looked around to see if anyone else was with him.

Colin and Tyler headed toward the door. Randall stood up, hesitated, then followed them. Then Cory stood up and left.

Jay just waited. No sense begging guys to stay.

"Do I mark these guys absent?" asked Brendan. "I

mean they were here, but not really for practice."

Jay knew what was on Brendan's mind. Coach Willis had a very strict rule about missing practices: one miss without an excuse got a warning; two misses got an automatic game suspension. "Could we just leave it for now? Maybe they'll change their minds and come back," Jay answered.

"It's my job to keep attendance," insisted Brendan.

"Yeah, you're right. Better mark them absent. They'll likely be here for next practice when Ms. Himmelman's here. Colin's just blowing off steam."

Brendan marked an X beside each of the four players' names, then went to the storage room and started throwing basketballs out into the gym.

"Okay!" shouted Jay. "Let's practise some ball control with the crossover dribble." He grabbed a basketball. "Remember to always use your fingertips, not your palm. Keep your head up."

"But aren't we supposed to do warm-ups first?" asked Steve.

"Oh, yeah. Right. Leave the balls! Make a circle!" Jay's throat was starting to feel dry and his confidence was slipping. "Sit-ups. Let's go for thirty." Jay led the guys through a quick warm-up routine, trying to go over in his mind some drills to do. He'd start with the give-and-go. Most of them pretty much knew how to do that.

But later, when he tried to explain the screen-away,

things got really tangled up. "Shooter is at the top of the circle and blocker comes in from the right," he said.

"Blocker's left," said Finn. "Passer's right."

"Right," said Jay. "Right. Passer's right." His confidence slipped further away. "So when the defender's blocked, the passer passes to the shooter or the blocker, whoever's set up for the shot." Did that make sense? It sounded to Jay as if his words were being tossed around in a pinball machine, just meaningless noise.

"Also," said Kyung, coming to the rescue, "the most important part of screen-away is perfect timing."

"Right," said Jay. "Timing."

The next hour crawled like a snail, with drills and scrimmages moving at the same slimy, slow pace. When Mr. Haley dropped by to see how things were going, he stayed only a few minutes. Jay figured he must have recognized that practice had disintegrated beyond the recovery point.

Hardly a word was spoken in the locker room afterward. Soon Kyung was the only one still there with Jay.

"That was a complete and total disaster," said Jay. "How am I supposed to do this? I can't even remember simple drills. And what about Colin and those guys walking out like that?"

"They will be back for the next practice."

"I'm not so sure. Colin's a real hothead these days. And if he doesn't come back, probably Tyler won't either. And maybe Cory and Randall."

"Not everyone is influenced by Colin."

"Well, they're sure not influenced by me."

"You are the team captain. That means they will respect you."

"Those guys probably didn't even vote for me." Jay stuffed his sneakers into his gym bag and hauled on his coat. "I couldn't even run a practice. You saw what happened. So how am I supposed to hold the team together? If something doesn't change fast, the Rockets are toast."

7 TURN IT AROUND

Before he finished his homework, Jay had made his decision. The whole problem was centred around Colin and that meant the solution had to be centred around him, too. If his negative attitude was because of Jay being team captain, then it could change to positive if Jay wasn't captain. Simple. The solution was for Colin to be team captain. All Jay had to do was tell Coach Willis he was stepping down and that whoever came second in the vote — probably Colin — should take over.

Jay picked up his cell phone and punched in the coach's number. "Mrs. Willis? Uh, this is Jay Hirtle from school. Coach Willis is my basketball coach. And I need to speak to him, please."

"Ed is sleeping, finally, and I really shouldn't disturb him," she said quietly. "He has been in so much discomfort, it's been impossible for him to even close his eyes."

Jay's shoulders sagged. If things were this bad, there wasn't much chance Coach Willis would be back for next practice. Or maybe even for the MacLeod game.

"I could ask Ed to return your call when he wakes up."

"That's okay, Mrs. Willis. He doesn't need to call. I just wanted to tell him that . . . that things went okay at practice today, so there's nothing to worry about."

"Thank you, Jay. Please call again. Ed will be happy to hear any news of his basketball team."

"Sure, okay."

"Goodbye, dear."

"Goodbye, Mrs. Willis."

Nothing to worry about. As if.

Coach Willis might think Jay was joking if he told him about players walking out of practice and leaving the rest of the team stranded. He would laugh out loud. *Ha ha ha. You're killin' me, Jay. What a comedian!*

But it was no joke.

Jay was on his own. He would have to move on his decision without help from Coach Willis. Talking to Colin wouldn't be easy, but so what? It'd be a breeze compared to what was going on already. And then the Rockets could get back to normal.

A bit of weight lifted from Jay's shoulders. Soon he wouldn't be team captain. He'd just be the Rockets' shooting guard. Plain and simple.

The next morning after he got off the bus, Jay didn't head directly into school. Instead, he waited for Colin's bus to arrive. He knew he'd have to talk fast to get his whole idea out before Colin walked away. The bus door opened and people started streaming out. Colin always sat at the back, so Jay knew he'd be one of the last ones out.

"I need to talk to you," Jay said as Colin stepped off the bus.

"I don't need to talk to you."

"You should —"

"You can't tell me what I should do," said Colin. "I'll do what I want. If I want to be at practice, I will. If I don't, then I won't. You think you can boss people around just 'cause you're team captain?"

"That's not what I —"

But Colin had already walked away.

★ ★ ★

Brendan was opening the storage room when Jay got to the gym at the end of the day. "Hi, Jay. How's it going?"

"Not too good."

"You think those guys'll come to practice?"

"I'm not sure."

"If they miss another practice, it's automatic suspension for the MacLeod game. They know Coach's rule."

"Yeah." *Unless we don't tell anyone they missed yesterday's practice*, thought Jay. "I called Coach last night but he was asleep. Mrs. Willis said he wasn't doing so good. Likely he won't be back for the MacLeod game tomorrow."

"You think we can do okay without him?"

"Maybe. We'll see how practice goes. Have you seen Ms. Himmelman?"

"Not yet." Brendan tossed basketballs out of the storage room and they rolled across the gym floor. "Hey, look."

Some of the players were coming out of the locker room. With them were Randall and Cory. Then Tyler walked into the gym. But Colin was nowhere in sight.

Jay picked up a basketball and walked over to Randall and Cory. "Thanks for coming to practice, guys," he said.

"Sorry about —"

"Forget yesterday, Randall. It's finished." Jay tossed the basketball to Cory. "No hard feelings. Let's just get on with playing the game."

He turned to find Tyler doing layups by himself at the end of the court. When he got close to the key, Jay switched into basketball play and cut in front of Tyler, blocking his shot. They both went up for the rebound. Jay tipped the ball and Tyler scrambled to get it. He dribbled, faced the basket, and made his shot count.

"Glad you're back," said Jay, and offered Tyler a high-five.

Tyler hesitated, then slapped Jay's palm. It didn't have much power behind it, but it was a start.

The mood wasn't great, but at least everyone was doing warm-ups: dribbling or shooting or getting rebounds. It looked like a basketball practice. It sounded like a basketball practice. For Jay, that was good enough.

Ms. Himmelman entered the gym and walked over to Jay and Brendan. "How's things going, boys?" She glanced around. "Everyone here?"

"Uh . . ." Brendan looked at Jay, then down at his clipboard. "Colin's not here yet."

She looked at her watch. "And he didn't speak to you about needing to be late or missing this practice?"

"No." Brendan was obviously not comfortable holding back what he knew.

Why try to cover things? thought Jay. *She's the coach for now. She has to know.* "Colin walked out of practice yesterday." He glanced at Brendan, who caught the hint to leave the other players out of it. They were back, so why complicate things?

"Walked out? What's up with that?" asked Ms. Himmelman.

"He just got mad and left," said Brendan.

"He's been uptight about some stuff lately," Jay said.

"I assume he's aware of the two-misses rule and the game suspension." Ms. Himmelman thought for a moment, then said, "Okay, I'm your interim coach and Ed's counting on me to do the same job I do with my girls' team. I'm not about to let him down. At the end of this practice, I'll be making a call home to Colin to inform him that he won't be playing tomorrow's game."

"Maybe he'll show up in a couple minutes," said Brendan.

Not a chance, thought Jay.

"If he does, we'll deal with it then. Now, how about I call your team together. Jay, you can give them an update on Coach Willis and maybe a bit of a pep talk for tomorrow's game." She clapped her hands to get everyone's attention. "Over here, boys! Find a spot on the floor and get comfortable."

Brendan sat down with the other guys, but Jay remained standing.

"As you know," Ms. Himmelman said, "I'm acting as your coach for this week while Coach Willis takes care of his leg injury. Despite the circumstances, I am very excited to have this chance to work with you. Now your team captain has a few things to say."

Everyone's eyes turned toward Jay.

The gym got very quiet.

Jay looked at each player in front of him. Brendan had his clipboard ready, as if Jay was about to say something worth writing down.

"Thanks for stepping in to be our coach, Ms. Himmelman. We really appreciate it. So does Coach Willis." Jay turned to face the team. "I called Coach's place last night. Didn't talk to him, but Mrs. Willis said he was doing okay. Guess his leg hurts a lot and he can't sleep. So anyway, we know he's counting on us for a win over MacLeod tomorrow."

Jay cleared his throat and tried to focus on making this pep talk work. "MacLeod gave us some good competition last year, especially in offence. We have to stop them under the basket. But no camping in the key and getting called for a violation. Our defence'll be how we win this game. And make sure when you're out there on the floor, you watch Tyler for plays. He's your point guard. Let's force a turnover whenever we can. Let's play a cautious game. No mistakes that cost us. I don't mean we're afraid to show what we can do. Just make every play work."

The pep talk didn't spark much enthusiasm.

Ms. Himmelman stepped forward. "Thanks, Jay. All good advice. Now, what drills will we start with today, guys? Dribbling? Pick-and-go? Layups?"

Jay glanced over at Brendan and remembered the defence video they had talked about. "How about defence? Brendan told me about this drill in a video he saw."

"Okay, Brendan, fill us in," she said.

Brendan put down his clipboard and quickly stood, rubbing his injured knee absent-mindedly as he always seemed to do.

Jay let his attention drift as Steve and Finn helped with Brendan's demonstration. Most of the stuff he'd said about the game strategy for tomorrow made sense. But every guy on the team knew that Colin was missing the second practice in a row and that meant they'd be playing against MacLeod without him — without their MVP.

But the day wasn't over. He had to be able to do something to fix this before the Rockets got on that bus and headed to MacLeod for their first basketball game of the season.

After practice, Jay didn't go to the locker room. "Ms. Himmelman? Could I talk to you for a minute?"

"Of course. Let's take a seat in Coach Willis's office."

It didn't take long for Jay to explain what was going on with Colin. Ms. Himmelman listened carefully, nodding a few times. Finally, she said, "You're asking me not to suspend him."

"Yeah. I mean, he showed up for practice yesterday. He just didn't stay. So in a way, you could say he just missed one whole practice."

Ms. Himmelman sighed. "I hear you." She looked around as if there might be an answer to the dilemma hanging on the walls of the coach's office. "Here's what I think," she said. "I think you're a fine team captain, Jay. The best. And I'll tell you why. You're putting aside your personal problems with Colin and you're putting your team first. You're trying to do whatever it takes to make your team strong. I respect that."

"We need a chance at the regionals, Ms. Himmelman. I don't think we can do that without Colin. He's our MVP."

"MVP? Not right now, he isn't. And I'm not

convinced he's got what it takes to turn himself around quickly enough, Jay. Unless you know something I don't."

"He never used to be like this. He used to be a team player, but . . . I don't know. It's like now he always has to be the number-one guy."

"I've seen this happen to players. They start out working solidly with the team and then they begin to believe every play and every success is dependent on their talents. They don't usually switch out of that me-first mode very easily, if at all."

"I at least have to try to turn things around. We need Colin on the team."

"So, what's your plan?"

"Give me a chance to talk to him before you do. If my plan works, maybe we can ignore the fact that he missed part of yesterday's practice and avoid the suspension."

Ms. Himmelman let a few seconds tick by on the clock above Coach Willis's desk. "Okay. You get back to me as soon as you've spoken to Colin. Let me know what happens." She stood up. "But I'm only giving you until this evening, Jay. If I'm going to be suspending Colin, I'll have to talk to Ed first because he's still your coach. He'll need to okay the decision. And then I'll make that call to Colin."

"Thanks, Ms. Himmelman. I really appreciate this. I mean it."

★ ★ ★

Night had started to settle in — no moon or stars — when Jay left his house and headed for Colin's. It was cold and damp, as if a soggy snowfall might be on the way. He pulled up the collar of his wool jacket and stuffed his hands into his pockets.

Just as he was about to ring the doorbell, the door opened and Colin's kid sister Shauna stepped quickly out.

"Oh! You scared me!" She had skates over her shoulder and her cell phone against her ear. "No, not you," she said into the phone. "Jay Hirtle did. He was standing right here when I walked out. Hold on a sec." She held the phone close to Jay's face. "Here, say hi to Diane. My new best friend."

"Uh . . . hi, Diane."

She put the phone to her ear again, but kept watching Jay. "Jay's way cute. Take a look." She took Jay's picture and sent it to her friend. "See? Am I right? You'd like him. Oh, now he's blushing. That's so sweet."

Jay brushed his fingers through his hair and turned away.

"Anyway, Colin's up in his room," Shauna said to Jay. "Video games, the usual. So one hundred per cent boring."

As Jay stepped into the front hall, he heard Shauna tell Diane she'd be at the rink in fifteen. What grade was

Shauna in, anyway? Six, maybe. How uncool was that, blushing because of something someone's kid sister said?

He shut the door behind him. "Hello?" he called out. He took a few steps toward the living room.

Colin's mother was reading under the light of a tall lamp, with the cat, Smudge, on her lap. "Jay! How nice to see you! I thought I heard Shauna talking to someone."

"Uh . . . she said Colin's in his room."

"Yes, go on up. You know the way. He's probably waiting for you."

Fat chance, thought Jay. "Okay, thanks."

At the top of the stairs, he hesitated. Then he stepped toward Colin's room and knocked on the door.

No answer.

Jay opened the door and walked in.

"What're you doing here?" asked Colin.

"I got this idea," said Jay quickly. "You should be team captain, not me. Coach said it was a close vote, anyway, and I figure you got way more votes than Mitchell."

"I'm suspended. How can I be captain?"

Jay was caught off guard. Did Ms. Himmelman go back on her word and make the call already? "Suspended?"

"Yeah. Think I don't know the rules? I missed two practices. I'm suspended."

"Did Ms. Himmelman call you?"

"Not yet, but she will. And who cares, anyway? It's only one game."

Colin didn't know how close Coach Willis was to cutting him from the team for good. "Look. You're not suspended. At least there's a chance you won't be because, in a way, you didn't miss a whole practice the other day. So Ms. Himmelman said she'd wait till I talked to you."

"She knows you're here?"

"Yes."

"And she knows you're saying I should be team captain?"

"No, I just said I had a plan and asked if I could talk to you about it."

"What about Coach Willis?"

"I didn't get a chance to say anything to him yet."

"He won't go along with it."

Jay could feel things shifting just slightly. There was less anger in Colin's words. Maybe he'll go along with this plan after all. "I'll say I don't want the job anymore and that it should go to whoever was closest in votes."

Suddenly, Colin's eyes darkened. "I don't need anyone handing me the team captain job. What's wrong? Why don't you want it? Can't handle the heat?"

Jay ignored the dig. "Coach Willis is counting on . . ." But he could see in Colin's eyes that none of that mattered. Not Coach Willis, not the Rockets, not the MacLeod game. He gave Colin a long, careful look, then left the room, closed the door, and slowly walked down the stairs.

"Do you need something, Jay?" Colin's mother came out of the living room, the open book in her hand. Smudge was close behind her.

"Uh . . . no thanks. I was just leaving."

"But you only arrived a few minutes ago."

"I just had to ask Colin something."

"Oh, well . . ."

There was an awkward silence. From the puzzled look on Colin's mother's face, Jay could see that she knew something was up but was trying not to interfere.

Colin came downstairs and into the kitchen, obviously not expecting Jay to still be there. The quiet got even quieter.

"Would you boys like some apple crisp? With ice cream?" asked Colin's mother.

"I'm full," said Colin. "We just ate."

"I should go," said Jay. "Thanks, though, Mrs. Hebb."

"I'm glad you came to visit. Even Smudge is glad to see you, aren't you, Smudge?" She tickled the cat's ears.

Jay bent down and patted the cat along its sleek back and out to the end of its long, grey tail. "How's it goin', Smudge?"

"She was Shauna's birthday gift six years ago last month. We got her from the animal rescue centre. All of us went together to pick her out. Remember, Colin?"

"Jay doesn't care about that stuff, Mom. He said he had to go."

"Everyone's in such a rush these days," sighed Colin's mother.

"I'm not really in a rush," said Jay. Then he caught the look Colin shot at him. "But I told Sam I'd help him with his math project."

"Oh, well, then you should be on your way. Sam's lucky to have a helpful big brother like you."

"What's that supposed to mean?" asked Colin. "Like I'm not a helpful brother?"

"I'm not saying that. What is wrong with you, Colin? I'm at my wits end. And don't for one minute think I can't see what's happened to your friendship with Jay. He hasn't visited you for months and now here he is making excuses to leave after barely ten minutes."

"Things change," said Colin. "Anyway, you guys can talk about the cat or anything else you want. I don't care. I have stuff to do." He left the kitchen and went back up the stairs, closing his bedroom door firmly behind him.

"Jay, I'm worried," Colin's mother said. "He really has changed. There's a negativity he didn't have before."

"I know."

"Has he fallen in with the wrong crowd?"

"I don't think so. I mean, he hangs out with Tyler, and Tyler's okay."

"But he doesn't bring Tyler here. Or anyone else. I

was glad to see you today. I thought —"

"I just had this idea for basketball I wanted to ask him about."

"I'm glad he's got basketball. It's very important to him. And being part of a team is just the experience he needs to bring him out of whatever this rut is he's in."

"Yeah, well . . ."

"His father and I have spoken to him about all this, but he doesn't have much to say. I'm not sure he listens to us. Friends tell us to be patient, that a lot of teens go through this phase. But I'm not so sure. Look at you — you're the same nice boy you've been since the day I met you. That's at least four years ago, isn't it?"

Jay shrugged his shoulders. "Uh, three, I guess." He was starting to feel really awkward, as if Colin might be at the top of the stairs listening.

"Look at me, keeping you from helping your little brother. You come back anytime, Jay."

"Sure. Okay, then. Bye, Mrs. Hebb."

As he walked toward home, Jay felt sorry he had lied to Colin's mother about helping Sam. He could've just said he had to go and leave it at that. No excuses. No lies. And it probably wasn't fair not saying something about Colin being suspended. Because that would happen now.

He had to go home and call Ms. Himmelman. From there, the ball would keep on rolling.

Everything was getting way too complicated.

8 GAME FACE

Jay felt as if he was holding his breath all day Thursday, waiting for the announcement to dismiss the basketball teams for their MacLeod games. The hands of the clock seemed frozen. Finally, the minute hand crawled from three-fourteen toward three-fifteen. Jay quietly stuffed his books into his backpack.

Then he heard the unmistakable click of the PA system: "Sorry for this interruption. Would teachers please excuse all members of the girls' and boys' basketball teams at this time? Players are asked to meet Ms. Himmelman at the front entrance. Thank you."

Jay was just ahead of Kyung as they left the classroom.

"Do not worry," said Kyung, smiling. "We will have a victory today."

He forced a smile, but it didn't match Kyung's. Jay was nervous. And why not? They were facing MacLeod with one of their best players missing. The whole team was aware of Colin's suspension and all the reasons behind it, not just the rule about missing two practices.

Having their MVP banned from the first game of the season could be enough to throw the Rockets off their game.

"I'll meet you on the bus," said Jay. "I just need to use the washroom."

He stepped into the boys' room and suddenly stopped, even before the door had closed behind him. Sitting alone on the tiled floor beneath the transom window was Colin. Beside him was his duffle bag of basketball gear. The image of a homeless teenager he'd seen in Halifax the winter before flashed into Jay's mind. The kid had been sitting on the sidewalk outside the Metro Centre when Sam and Jay and their dad came out after a Rainmen's basketball game. Their dad had given the homeless kid twenty dollars. Colin had the same dejected look as that homeless kid. It was almost a look of despair.

Colin reached for his basketball gear and quickly stood up. "I just —"

Jay suddenly realized what was going on. Colin had left his last class when the players were dismissed, avoiding questions that would expose his suspension. But no way could he show up at the front entrance with his basketball gear and get on the bus with everyone else. He was hiding.

"Look," said Jay, "it's okay. I get why you're here. I won't say anything to anyone. And I'm sorry about the suspension. I mean it."

A few shouts could be heard outside as players headed to the bus. Colin looked up at the open window, but said nothing.

"I better get going." Jay left the washroom as quickly as he'd entered, deciding he could wait until he got to the MacLeod locker room.

Brendan was at the front entrance, carrying two sports bags crammed with blue and white game balls for the warm-up, water bottles, towels, and oranges for halftime. Slung across one shoulder was a square black bag and stuffed under his arm was his clipboard.

"Got everything?" asked Jay.

"Yeah, and I borrowed a school video camera so we can replay some of the game next practice."

"Great idea." Jay hoped there'd be at least a few strong plays, though all he could think about was Colin. Just seeing him like that, sitting alone on the washroom floor. How different he looked from the friend Jay used to know.

Ms. Himmelman stood beside the bus as everyone climbed on. "Are all your players here, guys?"

"Yes," said Brendan. "I checked them off."

Jay noticed he didn't say, "Everyone except Colin."

"We have nine players," said Kyung as he stepped onto the bus. "We will win with nine."

"Great attitude there, Kyung," said Ms. Himmelman. "Keep it positive. That's the only way to succeed. I tell my girls that all the time." She did a last head count of everyone seated on the bus and turned to the driver. "Okay, Sue, we're ready to go."

Someone at the back yelled, "Who's gonna win?"

"We are!" came the chorus from both teams.

"Who's gonna lose?"

"MacLeod!"

"Who's gonna win?"

"We are!"

"Who's gonna lose?"

"MacLeod!"

"Who rules?"

"Rockets rule!"

Everyone was cheering and punching the air with their fists as the bus turned out of the driveway and headed toward Dr. A.C. MacLeod School for the first basketball games of the season. Jay was sure Colin could hear their cheers through that open window. That would be pretty depressing.

A few MacLeod fans were standing at the school entrance when the bus pulled up and the door clanged open. Some had their cheeks painted with green and gold stars, and all of them wore school sweatshirts.

One of the guys stepped forward. "Welcome to MacLeod, home of the Soaring Eagles!"

"Thank you very much!" said Ms. Himmelman with a wide smile. "A welcoming committee. How cool is that!"

"We can show you where the locker rooms are,"

said a girl with green and gold streaked hair.

"Well, we do know your school very well, having played here many times. But all the same, it would be nice to be escorted. Teams, let's follow these nice people," said Ms. Himmelman.

Jay grabbed a duffle bag as Brendan shifted the camera from one shoulder to the other.

"I will also help," said Kyung.

"That's okay," said Brendan. "I got everything now. Thanks."

"I will carry the camera."

"Okay, sure."

They walked into the school, past more MacLeod fans painted with gold and green stars. Finally, the Rockets arrived at the locker rooms.

"You boys'll be playing the first game. Let me know if you need anything," said Ms. Himmelman. "I'll knock on the door when it's time."

"Okay, thanks," said Brendan.

"I'm assuming your team has a warm-up worked out, Jay. Make an impression on those MacLeod fans."

"Uh . . . yeah, right," mumbled Jay.

"Good stuff." She went into the girls locker room, leaving Jay standing in the hall by himself.

Coach Willis always had warm-up drills before every game, but Jay had forgotten about that. He'd need to do a last-minute reminder, especially for the new guys. The bit of confidence he had was starting to shrink, and a sharp pain of anxiety sliced through his gut. His very first game as team captain was doomed.

He stared at the door of the locker room. There were eight players in there and they were counting on him to keep things together. Right now, what was important was concentrating on the team. All that mattered was a basketball court, a scoreboard, and two teams ready to play the first game of the basketball season. He was still the team captain. He had to do the best job he could.

He stepped toward the boys' locker room and pushed the door open.

Jay cleared his throat and glued a serious expression on his face. "Before you guys finish getting changed, let's just run through a few ideas for our warm-up. First, we do one lap around the gym and then make a circle in the centre. Tyler, you lead. Brendan, give me a game ball. Okay, thanks. When we're in the circle, I'll start with a dozen quick chest passes around the circle. And we'll make it noisy. I'll call out names. As each of you catches the ball, yell out numbers one to twelve. Then we'll break the circle and run in a line to the key for layups. Kyung, you lead the break and make the first layup. Next guy goes up for the rebound and passes the ball out. If anyone drops a ball, let it go. Brendan'll throw you another one and he'll get the ball that rolled. After that, we'll do some shots from the top of the key. Okay, let's get ready for the game."

Jay changed his clothes, going over the warm-up

routine and trying to think of some basic game strategies that always worked. When Ms. Himmelman knocked on the locker room door, he almost jumped.

Before they left the locker room, the Rockets gathered in a close circle, hand over hand.

"Who's gonna win!" yelled Jay.

"We are!"

"Who's gonna lose!"

"MacLeod!"

"Who rules!"

"Rockets rule!"

Jay held the door open. He slapped each player on the back as they passed him. "Let's win this one for Coach Willis!"

When everyone was out of the locker room, he let the door close and jogged into the gym behind his team.

★ ★ ★

At halftime, the Rockets were trailing MacLeod by three baskets with the score at 36 to 30. The plays were uneven, as if everyone on both teams couldn't get into the game and make things work the way they were supposed to. Even the MacLeod fans were quiet.

"I need your attention, boys. We only have a few minutes," said Ms. Himmelman as the Rockets gathered in the boys' locker room. "There are just six points between you and your win over MacLeod. I think you can handle that, no problem."

Jay didn't see the same confidence on the faces of his teammates. They were probably thinking about Colin and all the great plays that had earned him the MVP honour. And about the suspension that kept him out of this game.

"Tyler, you're doing a fine job as point guard," Ms. Himmelman continued, "calling plays and keeping your team focused. Now I want everyone to start feeding the ball to Cory. Kyung and Finn, you guys block MacLeod's defence and keep a path open for Cory straight to their basket. Jay and Tyler will be there for the rebound if we don't score. If you can close that six-point gap before the last quarter, you'll shake up MacLeod and the game will be yours."

Brendan passed around oranges and refilled water bottles.

"We'll call Coach Willis as soon as this game has ended and tell him about your win!" said Ms. Himmelman enthusiastically. "Jay, anything to add as the captain of your team?"

Jay wasn't as sure the game would be theirs, though he wouldn't say that out loud. He knew that one of the best ways to rally a team out of a slump at halftime was to keep things positive. "MacLeod's luck is about to turn," he said. "They're getting rattled and we're gonna keep it that way. A few fumbles in the first half cost us and gave them the edge. Let's control this second half. Like Ms. Himmelman says, this game's ours."

"Okay, guys. It's time," said Brendan.

The players formed a circle, hands piled on hands, and cheered, "GO-O-O-O-O, Rockets!"

Tyler led the first lineup onto the basketball court and stood at centre, ready to make the jump. The other four got into position. The players on the bench leaned forward to catch every move on the floor.

Through the second half, the scoreboard numbers flashed and changed — time drained away and the score slid slowly upward, always in favour of MacLeod. Despite their best attempts, Richmond continued to trail behind.

With three minutes and forty-one seconds left in the game, the score was 63–61 for MacLeod. The Rockets were getting tired and Jay knew it.

Ms. Himmelman called a time out.

"The three-point arc will save the Rockets," said Kyung before she had a chance to speak.

Everyone turned toward Kyung. "Randall can score from the three-point line," he said. "He is reliable."

"But MacLeod's defence is all over us," said Jay. "They won't risk losing their lead. If we've got the ball anywhere in the three-point arc, they'll swarm our player."

"I have a strategy," said Kyung.

"Okay. Let's hear it," said Ms. Himmelman.

"They see we are now feeding the ball to Cory. They will be watching Cory. We will feed the ball to Randall instead. But we will not let them force a long pass because we will lose the ball."

"So where am I?" asked Randall. "Top of the key?"

"Not there. You will be inside the key like you will do a layup. But suddenly, you cut to the three-point line. They will not expect this strategy. We do not pass to Cory. We pass to you — a short pass — and you make the shot. Three points."

"What's your take on this, Jay?" said Ms. Himmelman. "Think it'll work?"

In his mind, Jay slowly went over every detail of Kyung's strategy. He couldn't find any holes in it. "Let's go with it. You up for this, Randall?"

"Worth a try," he said.

"Okay, then. Finn, I'll take you off and put Randall in," said Ms. Himmelman. "Tyler, it's your ball."

Tyler took the ball outside under the basket, studying everyone in front of him. Randall was closest, inside the key. His guard blocked him. Kyung led his guard on a wild goose chase across the top of the key and away from Randall. Tyler watched Jay for a couple of seconds, but his guard was on him like glue, and now Randall's guard had moved over, ready to double-up on defence. Kyung shouted from the other side. Tyler made a quick bounce pass out to him and then ran up the centre of the key.

Cory pivoted away from his guard and gave an exaggerated shout for the ball. Kyung faked a pass to Cory, but sent the ball back to Tyler. Before Cory's guards could switch focus, Tyler pivoted and made the short pass to Randall, who was on the three-point line, his guard not quite back in position yet. Randall leaped, sending the ball into the air. *Swish!* The net trembled as the basketball fell cleanly through.

The Rockets swarmed Randall, hugging and cheering. When they released him, he gave Kyung a solid high-five. "Way to go! It worked!"

"We worked!" yelled Kyung.

The referee's whistle blew. "Time out, MacLeod."

The Rockets made a circle in front of their bench, still high with the thrill of that last play.

"That was perfect," said Jay. "Perfect!"

"I got the whole thing right here!" said Brendan, holding the video camera above his head. "The whole thing!"

"Post it on YouTube!" said Finn.

"Right! Soon as I get home, I'll do it! This'll go viral!"

Ms. Himmelman pulled everyone's attention back to the job still to be done. "There's one minute and twenty-two seconds left. You have to stall. It's your only choice. They need to score. That's what they're talking about over there right now. Look for fakes. Look for long shots. Do what you have to and get the ball back. Then stall."

As the MacLeod players jogged onto the basketball court, Jay could see that every one of them was determined to give the home fans the victory they wanted. The bleachers were alive with green and gold banners, waving arms, and cheering voices: "Go, MacLeod, go! Go, MacLeod, go!"

The long pass from outside was rock-solid and MacLeod was suddenly racing toward the Rockets' basket. Tyler just as suddenly made a wall in front of the MacLeod forward, forcing him to pass the ball to the player behind him. Randall cut sharply and intercepted.

Rockets' ball.

Jay glanced at the clock — fifty-seven seconds. But that glance cost them — he didn't see Randall's quick pass until it was too late. The ball ricocheted off Jay's hand and rolled.

Kyung threw himself on the basketball as if he was on a football field. A MacLeod player slid to the floor, claiming the ball at the same time.

The referee blew the whistle. "Jump!"

Jumps were definitely not one of Kyung's strengths. His face clouded with worry.

Jay walked over and gave his friend a reassuring pat on the back. "We got you covered," he said.

Kyung pushed his sweatband higher up on his forehead, ran his fingers down his face, and wiped his hands on the back of his shorts. He took a couple of deep breaths. Without even glancing at the MacLeod centre, he positioned himself for the jump and concentrated on the ball held high in the ref's hand.

The referee made the toss.

The MacLeod player tipped the ball, but the force sent it soaring above the players' heads. It bounced across the sideline.

The referee's whistle blew again. "Rockets' ball."

The time showed seventeen seconds remaining. The score: 63 Home, 64 Visitors.

"You guys know what to do!" shouted Tyler.

And everyone did. Stall, stall, stall.

Kyung took the ball out of bounds. He spun it between his hands, then bounced it hard once.

Cory and Randall criss-crossed the key, their guards staying right with them. Jay was open and easily received Kyung's bounce pass from the sidelines.

"Okay, slow it down," yelled Tyler.

Holding one arm wide to keep his guard away from the ball, Jay dribbled steadily, barely moving down the court. He didn't chance looking at the clock.

The MacLeod defence was tight. Jay knew they would've figured out the Rockets' stalling tactic. With nothing to lose, they might make a grab for the ball, even if they risked a foul.

Jay had barely formed this thought when his guard moved in and tipped the ball out of his hands. The guard pivoted and made a wild shot toward the Rockets' basket. Jay lurched to block the shot. He was thrown off balance and fell against his guard. They both toppled.

The whistle blew and the referee pointed at Jay. "Rockets' foul, seventeen, charging."

Jay scrambled to his feet and helped the MacLeod player sprawled on the floor get back up. "Sorry about that," he said.

His opponent grinned. "No problem. Thanks for the chance to score a couple of foul shots."

He was right. Two free throws would clinch the game for MacLeod. Jay looked over at Tyler, who was trying to keep a neutral look on his face. The other players were already in position around the key. Ms. Himmelman was standing up beside the bench, one hand across her mouth.

The clock showed six seconds. Useless. After MacLeod scored their free throws, the game would be over before the Rockets could execute a single pass.

The MacLeod fans became very quiet.

The referee tossed the ball to the MacLeod player at the top of the key.

He set his feet in position, spread his fingers across the back of the ball, and lined up the ball with the basket. He jumped and made the shot. The ball swished against the bottom of the net and hit the back wall.

A groan of disappointment came from the bleachers.

"Take your time!" shouted the MacLeod coach.

A tie was still possible. Jay could see that the MacLeod player was rattled.

The player in green and gold held the ball against his chest and took a couple of deep breaths. Then he wiped his forehead and eyes with the back of his wrist. He bounced the ball five times — low, quick bounces. He caught it, then bounced once more. He went up for the shot. Before the basketball left his hands, his foot slipped over the free-throw line. Violation. The referee made the call.

As the whistle blew, the ball tapped the backboard and slipped through the hoop. Some MacLeod fans weren't paying attention and cheered. But the scoreboard didn't change: 63 Home, 64 Visitors.

Four seconds left.

Jay took the ball out under the basket. He passed it quickly to Kyung, who made the return pass as Jay ran into the key. The ball was still in his hands when the buzzer ended the game. Pandemonium! The Rockets cheered and hugged and gave high-fives as though they'd just won the season championship.

"Rockets rule!" Kyung yelled to Jay inside the crush of players.

Ms. Himmelman was on her cell phone to Coach Willis in minutes. "We won 64 to 63! Yeah, yeah . . . a three-point basket with about a minute to go!" She covered one ear with her palm, trying to hear Coach Willis over the excitement bursting all around. "Randall scored with a pass from Tyler! Brendan got it all on video!" She waved Jay over. "Coach wants to talk to you!"

Jay put the phone to his ear. "Hi, Coach."

"Sounds like you guys pulled off quite the finale in this game."

"Yeah, well, Randall did. And it was Kyung's idea to go for the three-point basket. He planned the fake strategy, too. We switched focus from Cory to Randall, and MacLeod didn't catch on in time to block us. Brendan's gonna post the play on YouTube as soon as he gets home. You'll be able to check it out."

"I know you started out with a disadvantage this afternoon," he said.

Jay knew he was avoiding saying Colin's name. This wasn't the time to talk about the suspension. "Yeah."

"You did a great job, Jay. We couldn't have a better captain digging in there for the Rockets and making it happen."

"Thanks, Coach," Jay said. It sure wasn't the time to talk about giving up the job of team captain, either. "I better get back with the guys. Yeah . . . sure . . . okay, I'll tell them. Here's Ms. Himmelman. Bye, Coach." He passed the cell phone back.

"You missed an awesome basketball game, Ed!" said Ms. Himmelman into the phone. "Can't say enough about your boys — they did our school proud!"

As the Richmond boys watched the girls' game from the bleachers, Jay felt the victory mood gradually fade. The girls team maintained a strong advantage over MacLeod throughout their game. And when the game ended, their win wasn't because of a fluke. They could confidently move on to their next game and the next and the next, until they played in the regionals and maybe even brought home another basketball banner to hang in the Richmond gym — just like they did the year before.

Jay knew that his Rockets couldn't do the same unless they played every game together as a team. Unless they *all* played every game together as a team. Colin wouldn't buy into that. And one negative player could infect the whole team.

Unless Jay did something about this situation, there would not be a new boys' basketball banner on the Richmond gym wall at the end of the season.

9 WINNING COMBINATION

"I left today's paper there on the table for you," said Jay's dad. "Thought you'd be interested in the cover story."

Jay popped his dinner into the microwave and walked over to the kitchen table.

The photo on the front page of the newspaper showed a basketball player with his daughter, a preschooler, sitting on his shoulders. They were in a gym, each holding a basketball, though hers was a lot smaller than regulation size.

Jay picked up the paper.

"Remember that guy? He plays for the Halifax Rainmen," said his dad. "Guess he did a complete one-eighty turnaround a couple seasons ago and saved his basketball career." He filled the coffee grinder with beans, and then pressed the ON button. "This might be something you'd want your guys to see. Since you're team captain. You know — as inspiration."

Jay started to read the article as he ate his warmed-up lasagna.

The Rainmen's power forward had been suspended from the team a few years before. He had been mouthing off at refs, ignoring his coach, and not much caring about what he did on or off the court. Near the bottom of the column was a quote from the basketball player: *"It was me first and whoever second. I didn't care about anybody but myself."*

The story was beginning to sound familiar to Jay. With just a few changes in basic details, the article could've been about Colin. At least, about the kind of guy Colin had been lately.

Jay read on. The player had been suspended for the season after mouthing off one-too-many times and having a major disagreement with the coach. Colin didn't argue with Coach Willis, and his suspension was for one game, not a whole season — but the pattern was definitely there. Both guys were acting self-centred and negative.

It was there the similarities stopped. The guy in the article had made a big turnaround — he became a true team player, even becoming co-captain for the Rainmen.

The last paragraph of the article gave the owner and general manager of the Rainmen the final word: *"He's leading by example. He has matured as a person and we're glad he's still here."*

"Nice human-interest story," said Jay's dad as he leaned against the kitchen counter, waiting for coffee to finish dripping into the pot. "A player comes into a team thinking he's the number-one guy and not caring about anyone else. Till he gets a wake-up call. That player could've ended his basketball career before he was barely started."

"Why do you think he changed?"

"Probably a lot of things contributed. But I'd say the manager's attitude played a big part. When the coach suspended that player, the manager decided to offer him a second chance. Maybe people don't always show it, but when they mess things up in their lives, I'm sure they're aware of every depressing detail."

"It's kind of like one day they look in a mirror and see what they've really been like," said Jay.

"You've got that right. Sometimes all it takes is an offer from someone who wants them to succeed. And, if they're smart, they'll take the offer and switch things up in their lives."

All of a sudden, one word from the newspaper article popped into Jay's mind. *Co-captain.* And he knew he had the solution to the Rockets' troubles. "Dad, I have to go over to Colin's," he said, taking a last gulp of milk.

"Now? Isn't it a bit late for —"

"It's important."

"Couldn't you call?"

"This needs to be face-to-face, Dad. In person." Jay put his dishes in the dishwasher and went to the hall closet for his coat.

"I'll drive you over when your mom gets home. She'll stay with Sam."

"Mom's probably going to be late. Someone's having a baby or there's an emergency or something." Jay hauled on his jacked and grabbed a scarf.

"I can babysit myself." Sam stood at the top of the stairs with Rudy beside him.

"What if a burglar crashes in and ties you up and locks you in the closet and steals all your toys?" said Jay.

"Rudy will bite him."

"Then Rudy'll get arrested and the burglar will sue for damages."

Sam thought about Jay's words for a few seconds. He patted Rudy, then sat down on the top step with one arm across the dog's back.

"I won't be long, Dad. I'll likely be home before Mom." As Jay closed the door, he heard Sam asking his father something about lawyers for dogs.

★ ★ ★

For the second time in two days, Jay stood on the Hebbs' front step, uninvited. He rang the doorbell.

Colin opened the door, then started to close it again.

"Wait!" said Jay. "Give me a chance to talk."

"If this is about me being in the washroom —"

"It isn't! Forget that. I have to ask you something important."

Shauna came into the front hall. "Hey, saw that clip of your basketball game on YouTube. Everyone's watching it. You on Facebook? Diane wants to friend you."

"You know Diane?" Colin asked Jay.

"Not really, I —"

"I introduced them yesterday on my phone," Shauna said. "And Diane thinks Jay's cute." She grinned and walked away.

Colin gave Jay a weird look. "Diane's maybe twelve."

Why even try to explain? Jay switched the topic. "Did you see the video clip?"

"Yeah, I saw it."

Was Colin actually impressed by the clip? Jay couldn't tell by the expression on his face. Colin was still holding the door. Jay was still standing outside. He knew if he waited any longer to say what he'd come there to say, he'd be staring at a closed door.

"I want you to take on the job of co-captain of the Rockets." Jay didn't give Colin a chance to interrupt. "We'll have different roles. You'll do team strategies and help with things players need to work on. I'll do team awareness and pep talks, stuff like that. Lots of teams have co-captains."

"But you won the vote."

"Coach said the vote was really close. It makes sense to have co-captains." For a couple of seconds, Colin didn't say anything. Then he stepped outside and closed the door behind him. "How come you're doing this?"

"I promised myself the Rockets would get that regional championship banner this year. Centreville's got too many of them. This one's ours."

"What's that got to do with me being co-captain?"

"I gotta say this straight up. You're —" Jay wanted to make sure every word was exactly right. "Things aren't going that good for the Rockets, even if we did win our game today. Part of it's because you got suspended. That started the season off on the wrong track." He took a deep breath. "And if we're co-captains, maybe things'll smooth out for the team. Give us all a chance to concentrate on playing our best basketball."

Colin looked down, not making eye contact with Jay. "I didn't think you guys had a chance against MacLeod if I wasn't playing."

"The win was a fluke."

"That play was no fluke."

"We couldn't pull it off again. Not unless things get back to normal and the team gets a chance to really gel. Right now, things are all over the place."

Colin rubbed the back of his neck nervously. "Coach Willis called me tonight after I got suspended by Ms. Himmelman. He said he was one hundred per cent behind her decision. He told me if I didn't change my attitude, I'd be off the team for good and he'd find a replacement. He wasn't joking." Colin stared up at the light over the door, then turned back to Jay. "I mean, it's pretty bad hiding in a washroom while everyone else is heading out to play basketball. I felt like such a loser."

"That's not —"

"I don't know what I'd do if I really got kicked off the team."

"So don't get kicked off the team, then. It's your call. If you're co-captain, it'll show Coach you're working on changing and making things better for the team."

"Why should Coach Willis say yes to me being co-captain?"

"He plays fair. He'll let you have this chance to show what you can do. Besides, if he thinks this'll help the Rockets, he'll want to give it a try."

"What about the guys on the team? You sure they'll be okay with this?"

"Like I already said, a lot of them voted for you anyway. And I'm still a captain, so the guys who voted for me will be cool with it, too. It's a win–win situation. So are you in or not?"

Colin seemed to think through every detail of their conversation. Finally, he nodded his head slowly and smiled. "I don't get it, though. After all the stuff I did, you still want me for co-captain. You're nuts!"

"I'll take that as a *yes*," said Jay, grinning. "We'll call a team meeting tomorrow so the guys can meet their new co-captain."

On his way back home, Jay was feeling really good. He'd finally accomplished something for the Rockets.

At least he wasn't a complete write-off as team captain. If the guys thought he was copping out by giving away half his responsibilities, he'd just have to accept that. The co-captain idea was definitely going to work, and soon the team would get back to normal.

"Jay!" The shout came from the other side of the street. Kyung waited for a car to pass, then jogged across. "I did not expect to see you."

"Just heading home."

"Me too. I was at Finn's house watching our play on YouTube. One hundred times." He laughed. "I have sent it to Min Ki and he will be very impressed. He will show it to his team, I know for sure."

"Seoul, Korea, watching Richmond, Nova Scotia. Too cool," said Jay.

"I am making a Rockets Facebook page with Finn. First to introduce all the Rockets players and second to post updates during the basketball season. It will be excellent!"

"Hey, great! Maybe the first part could be something like the Knights promo. Action shots of everyone and special effects and everything. That promo's awesome."

Kyung grinned. "I have watched that a hundred times, too."

"I was just over at Colin's," said Jay.

There was a quick shift in Kyung's mood, but he didn't say anything. "It was okay. Really. I . . ." Though he wasn't sure what Kyung's reaction would be, there was no sense holding back. "I asked Colin to be co-captain and he said yes."

"Does Coach Willis know?"

"Not yet. I'll call him in the morning. He'll be okay with it." He decided not to mention that Colin had been warned he could get kicked off the team. Why spread stuff like that about the Rockets' new co-captain?

"I know why you are doing this," said Kyung. "You are helping the Rockets by making sure that Colin will change from negative to positive."

"Something like that."

"When I nominated you for team captain, I did a very good thing." Kyung grinned, then started back across the quiet street. "I will see you in homeroom tomorrow!"

"Okay. See ya." When Kyung got to the other side, Jay shouted, "And thanks! Not just for the nomination. For all kinds of stuff!"

Kyung waved. "No problem!"

As he walked along, Jay could see the flash and flicker of wide-screen TVs in some living rooms. Other homes were already darkened and everyone in bed. Nearing home, he noticed his mother's car still wasn't in their driveway. His dad would be waiting up for her, and Sam would be in bed, already sound asleep.

"How'd your visit go?" asked his dad.

"Good."

"Just good? Seemed like something pretty important was up when you left here."

"Yeah, well, it all worked out." Later, he'd fill his dad in on the co-captain deal he made with Colin and all the reasons why. Right now, he had one more very important thing to do.

As Jay passed Sam's room, Rudy lifted his head and looked out, then resumed his sprawl across the bottom of Sam's bed.

Jay opened his laptop and typed a quick message to Mike Murphy: *Check this out. The banner's ours! Rockets rule!* He added the YouTube video link and pressed SEND.

Jay grinned, picturing Mike getting that message and having a good laugh. At first. *Just a bit of competitive fun between team captains, right?* But at the next Cougars practice, Mike would get his team working on new strategies — a few surprises to hype up their first game against the Rockets.

Whatever Mike and his Cougars did, they'd be wasting their time. This year, the Rockets had the winning combination. Jay could already see the basketball championship banner hanging on the wall in the Richmond Academy gym.